PENGUIN BOOKS

MAIGRET MEETS A MILORD

Georges Simenon was born at Liège in
Belgium in 1903. At sixteen he began work
as a journalist on the *Gazette de Liège*. He has
published over 175 books, many of them
psychological novels, and others in the
Inspector Maigret series, and his work has
been admired by almost all the leading
French and English critics. His books have
been translated into more than twenty-five
languages and more than forty of them have
been filmed; his psychological novels have
had a great influence on the French cinema.
He has travelled all over the world, and at
one time lived on a cutter making long
journeys of exploration round the coasts of
Northern Europe. He is married and has four
children. His recreations are riding, fishing,
and golf.

GEORGES SIMENON

MAIGRET MEETS A MILORD

*

TRANSLATED
BY ROBERT BALDICK

PENGUIN BOOKS

Penguin Books Ltd, Harmondsworth, Middlesex, England
Penguin Books Inc., 7110 Ambassador Road, Baltimore, Maryland 21207, U.S.A.
Penguin Books Australia Ltd, Ringwood, Victoria, Australia
Penguin Books Canada Ltd, 41 Steelcase Road West, Markham, Ontario, Canada

—

Le Charretier de la 'Providence' first published 1931
This translation first published 1963 in Penguin Books
Reprinted 1964, 1970, 1972, 1974

—

Copyright © A. Fayard et Cie, 1931
Translation copyright © the Estate of Robert Baldick, 1963

—

Made and printed in Great Britain
by Cox & Wyman Ltd, London,
Reading and Fakenham
Set in Monotype Garamond

CHAPTER I

Lock 14

NOTHING could be deduced from the most minute recon-
struction of the facts, except that the find by the two carters
from Dizy was so to speak impossible.

That Sunday – it was the 4th of April – the rain had
started pouring down at three o'clock in the afternoon.

At that time, in the port above Lock 14, which marked
the junction between the Marne and the canal, there were
two motor-barges going downstream, one boat unloading,
and a dredger.

Shortly before seven o'clock, when dusk was beginning
to fall, a tanker, the *Éco III*, had arrived and entered the
lock.

The lock-keeper had been in a bad temper, because some
relations of his had called. He had shaken his head at a
horse-barge which had arrived a minute later, moving at
the slow pace of its two nags.

Not long after he had gone back into his house, the
carter, a man he knew, had come in.

'Can I go through? The skipper wants to get to Juvigny
by tomorrow night.'

'You can go through if you like. But you'll have to work
the gates yourself.'

The rain was falling more and more heavily. From his
window, the lock-keeper saw the stocky figure of the carter
trudging from one gate to the other, urging his horses
forward, and fastening the mooring-ropes to the bollards.

The barge rose little by little above the walls. It was not
the skipper who was holding the wheel, but his wife, a fat
Brussels woman with peroxided hair and a shrill voice.

At twenty past seven the *Providence* was moored in front
of the Café de la Marine, behind the *Éco III*. The horses

were taken on board. The carter and the skipper made for the café, where there were some other seamen and two pilots from Dizy.

At eight o'clock, when darkness had fallen completely, a tug arrived at the gates with the four boats it had in tow.

This added to the company in the Café de la Marine. There were six tables occupied, with people calling from one table to another. The men coming in left puddles of water behind them and shook the mud off their boots.

In the next room, which was lit by an oil-lamp, the women were doing their shopping.

The air was heavy. There was talk of an accident which had occurred at Lock 8 and the delay which might be suffered by boats going upstream.

At nine o'clock the wife of the *Providence*'s skipper came to fetch her husband and the carter, who went off after farewells all round.

At ten o'clock the lights were out on board most of the boats. The lock-keeper accompanied his relations as far as the main road to Épernay, which crossed the canal two miles from the lock.

He saw nothing unusual. As he was passing the Café de la Marine on his way back, he looked inside and was hailed by a pilot.

'Come and have a drop! You're soaking wet . . .'

He had a rum, still standing. Two carters got to their feet, sluggish with red wine, their eyes shining, and made for the stable adjoining the café, where they slept on the straw, next to their horses.

They were not exactly drunk. But they had had enough wine to send them into a heavy sleep.

There were five horses in the stable, which was lit only by a storm-lantern with the wick turned down low.

At four o'clock one of the carters roused his companion and the two of them started attending to their horses. They heard the horses on the *Providence* being brought off the barge and harnessed.

6

At the same time the proprietor of the café was getting up and lighting the lamp in his bedroom, on the first floor. He too heard the *Providence* moving off.

At half past four the diesel engine of the tanker started spluttering, but it did not leave until a quarter of an hour later, after the skipper had drunk a hot toddy in the café, which had just opened.

He had scarcely gone out and his boat had not yet reached the bridge before the two carters made their find.

One of them was pulling his horses towards the tow-path. The other was rummaging in the hay for his whip when his hand came into contact with something cold.

Startled by the touch of what felt like a human face, he went to get his lantern, and cast its light over the corpse which was going to send Dizy into a turmoil and upset the whole life of the canal.

*

Chief-Inspector Maigret of the Flying Squad was recapitulating these facts and putting them in their context.

It was the Monday evening. In the morning the Épernay magistrates had made their statutory visit to the scene of the crime, and after the Records Office men and the police doctors had done their work, the corpse had been taken to the mortuary.

It was still raining, a fine, cold, steady rain which had gone on falling all night and throughout the day.

Silhouettes were moving about on the gates of the lock, in which a boat was rising imperceptibly.

During the hour that he had been there, the Chief-Inspector had thought of nothing but of how to familiarize himself with a world which he had suddenly discovered and about which, on his arrival, he had only vague, mistaken ideas.

The lock-keeper had told him:

'There was hardly anything in the canal reach: two motor-barges going downstream, one motor-barge going

7

upstream which made the lock in the afternoon, a dredger, and two Panamas. Then the kettle arrived with her four boats . . . .'

And Maigret had learnt that a kettle is a tug, and that a Panama is a boat which has neither an engine nor any horses on board but hires a carter with his horses for a given distance, an operation known as 'getting a snatch'.

Arriving at Dizy, he had seen nothing but a narrow canal, three miles from Épernay, and a small village near a stone bridge.

He had had to splash through the mud along the tow-path as far as the lock, which itself was two miles from Dizy.

And there he had found the lock-keeper's grey stone house with its signboard reading: 'Lock Office.'

And he had gone into the Café de la Marine, which was the only other building in the place.

On the left, a shabby bar-room, with brown oilcloth on the tables, and walls painted half brown, half dirty yellow.

But there was a characteristic scent in the air which was enough to distinguish the place from an ordinary country café. It smelt of stables and harness, tar and groceries, petrol and diesel oil.

The door on the right was fitted with a little bell and there were some transparent advertisements stuck on the glass panes.

The room behind was packed with goods for sale: oil-skins, clogs, linen garments, sacks of potatoes, barrels of cooking oil and crates of sugar, peas and beans, all mixed up with vegetables and crockery.

There was not a customer to be seen. In the stable the only horse left was the one the proprietor harnessed to go to market, a big grey animal as friendly as a dog, which was not tied up and occasionally ambled about the yard, among the hens.

Everything was streaming with rain. That was the dominant note. And the people passing by were dark, shining figures, bent forward.

A hundred yards away, a little Decauville train travelled backwards and forwards across a building yard, and its driver, at the back of the miniature engine, had fixed up an umbrella under which he was standing shivering, with his shoulders hunched up.

A barge moved away from the bank and punted along as far as the lock, from which another barge was emerging.

How had the woman got there, and why had she come? That was the question which the Épernay police, the officials from the Public Prosecutor's department, the doctors, and the technicians from the Records Office had asked themselves in amazement and which Maigret was turning over and over in his great head.

She had been strangled, that was one thing which was certain. Death had occurred on the Sunday evening, probably about half past ten.

And the corpse had been found in the stable shortly after four o'clock in the morning.

There was no road in the vicinity of the lock. Nothing could bring anybody there who was not concerned with navigation. The tow-path was too narrow for a motor-car. And that particular night, anybody walking along it would have had to wade up to his knees through mud and water.

But the woman obviously belonged to a class more accustomed to travelling in limousines and sleeping-cars than on foot.

She was wearing nothing but a cream-coloured silk dress and a pair of white buckskin shoes which were more suitable for the beach than for the town.

The dress was crumpled but they had not found a single mud-stain on it. Only the toe of the left shoe was still wet when the body was discovered.

'Between thirty-eight and forty,' the doctor had said after examining the woman.

Her ear-clips were two genuine pearls, worth about fifteen thousand francs. Her gold and platinum bracelet, shaped in an ultra-modern style, was ornate rather than expensive, but bore the signature of a jeweller in the Place Vendôme.

The hair was brown and waved, cut very short at the nape of the neck and at the temples.

As for the face, which had been disfigured by strangulation, it had obviously been remarkably pretty.

From all appearances a gay society woman.

Her finger-nails, which were manicured and polished, were dirty.

No handbag had been found near her. The police of Épernay, Rheims, and Paris had been provided with a photograph of the corpse and had been trying in vain all day to establish its identity.

And the rain went on falling relentlessly on an ugly landscape. To the left and right, the horizon was barred by chalky hills streaked with black and white, where the vines, at this time of the year, looked like wooden crosses in a war cemetery.

The lock-keeper, whose only mark of identity was a cap trimmed with silver braid, circled miserably round his lock, in which the water started bubbling every time he opened the sluices.

And every sailor, while a boat was rising or falling, had to listen as he told the story.

Sometimes the two men, once the necessary papers had been signed, strode into the Café de la Marine and had a glass of rum or a mug of white wine.

The lock-keeper never failed to jerk his chin towards Maigret who, prowling aimlessly around, must have given the impression that he was nonplussed.

It was a fact. The case was quite exceptional. There was not even a single witness to question.

For the officials from the Public Prosecutor's department, after questioning the lock-keeper and coming to an understanding with the local Government engineer, had decided to allow all the boats to continue on their way.

The two carters had been the last to leave, about midday, each convoying a 'Panama'.

As there was a lock every three or four miles, and as these locks were linked by telephone, it was possible to know at any given moment where any given boat was to be found and bar its way.

What was more, a police inspector from Épernay had questioned everybody, and Maigret had at his disposal the record of these interrogations from which nothing could be deduced, except that reality was improbable.

All the people who had been at the Café de la Marine the day before were known either to the proprietor or the lock-keeper, and more often than not to both.

The carters slept at least once a week in the same stable, and always in the same condition bordering on intoxication.

'You see, we have a drink at every lock. . . . Nearly every lock-keeper sells wine. . . .'

The tanker which had arrived on Sunday afternoon and left on Monday morning was carrying petrol and belonged to a big company in Le Havre.

As for the *Providence*, whose skipper was also her owner, she went through twenty times a year, with her two horses and her old carter. And the same was true of the others.

Maigret was in a grumpy mood. A hundred times he went into the stable, then into the café or the shop.

He was seen walking as far as the stone bridge and giving the impression of counting his steps or looking for something in the mud.

With a scowl on his face, and dripping with water, he watched a dozen boats go through the lock.

People wondered what his theory was, but in fact he had none. He was not even trying to find a clue properly speaking, but rather to steep himself in the atmosphere, to familiarize himself with this canal life which was so different from all that he knew.

He had made sure that he could borrow a bicycle if he wanted to catch up with one or other of the boats.

The lock-keeper had lent him the *Official Handbook to Inland Navigation*, in which obscure places like Dizy took on an unexpected importance for topographical reasons, or on account of a junction, a crossing, or the presence of a port, a crane, even an office.

He tried to follow in imagination barges and carters:

'*Ay: Port. Lock 13.*'

'*Mareuil-sur-Ay: Boat-building yard. Port.*'

'*Lock 12. . . .*'

Then '*Bisseuil. Tours-sur-Marne, Condé, Aigny. . . .*'

At the far end of the canal, beyond the Langres plateau, which the boats mounted lock by lock and went down on the opposite slope, the Saône, Chalon, Mâcon, Lyons. . . .

'What was that woman doing here?'

In a stable, with her pearl ear-clips, her stylish bracelet, her white buckskin shoes.

She must have arrived alive, since the crime had been committed after ten o'clock at night.

But how? But why? And nobody had heard a thing. She had not screamed. The two carters had not woken up.

If it had not been for the whip which had been mislaid, the corpse would probably have been found only a fortnight or a month later, accidentally, by someone poking about in the hay.

And other carters would have come and snored beside that woman's body.

In spite of the cold rain, there was still something heavy and implacable about the atmosphere. And the rhythm of life was slow.

Feet in boots or clogs trailed across the walls of the lock or along the tow-path. Dripping horses waited for the end of the locking to move off again, straining forward in a repeated effort and thrusting back with their hind-legs.

And dusk was about to fall, just like the day before. Already the barges going upstream were not continuing on their way but mooring for the night, while the bargees were sluggishly making their way in groups towards the café.

Maigret went to have a look at the bedroom which had just been prepared for him next to the proprietor's. He stayed there for ten minutes or so, changed his shoes, and cleaned his pipe.

Just as he was going downstairs a yacht steered by a seaman in oilskins moved gently along beside the bank, went astern, and came smoothly to a stop between a couple of bitts.

The seaman carried out all these manoeuvres by himself. Two men came out of the cabin a little later, glanced wearily around them, and finally made for the Café de la Marine.

They too were wearing oilskins. But when they took them off they were seen to be dressed in open-necked flannel shirts and white trousers.

The bargees looked at the new-comers without causing them the slightest embarrassment. On the contrary, this sort of surroundings seemed to be familiar to them.

One of them was a tall, heavily-built man with greying hair, a brick-coloured complexion, and prominent sea-green eyes with a gaze which slid over people and things as if it did not see them.

He leant back on his straw-bottomed chair, pulled a second chair towards him for his feet, and snapped his fingers to call the proprietor.

His companion, who must have been about twenty-five, was talking English to him with a nonchalance which savoured of snobbery.

It was he who asked without any trace of an accent:

'Have you any still champagne?'

'Yes.'

'Bring us a bottle.'

They were smoking Turkish cigarettes with cardboard tips.

The bargees' conversation, which had been interrupted for a moment, gradually started up again.

Shortly after the proprietor had brought the wine, the seaman came in, dressed in white trousers too, with a sailor's blue-striped jersey.

'Over here, Vladimir. . . .'

The bigger of the two men yawned, displaying a massive boredom. He drained his glass with a grimace which was only half-satisfied.

'Another bottle!' he whispered to the younger man.

And the other repeated in a louder voice, as if he was accustomed to transmitting orders in that way:

'Another bottle! . . . The same again!'

Maigret came out of his corner, where he had been sitting in front of a bottle of beer.

'Excuse me, gentlemen. . . . May I ask you a question?'

The older man pointed to his companion with a gesture which signified:

'Ask him!'

He showed neither surprise nor interest. The seaman poured himself a drink and cut off the end of a cigar.

'You've come here by way of the Marne?'

'Yes, of course.'

'Were you moored a long way from here last night?'

The big fellow turned his head and said in English:

'Tell him that's no business of his.'

Maigret pretended not to have understood, and without saying anything more, took the photograph of the corpse out of his wallet and placed it on the brown oilcloth on the table.

The bargees, sitting at the tables or standing in front of the bar, were following the scene with their eyes.

The yachtsman scarcely moved his head to look at the photograph. Then he examined Maigret and sighed:

'Police?'

He had a pronounced English accent and a tired voice.

'Yes. A murder was committed here last night. So far it hasn't been possible to identify the victim.'

'Where is she?' asked the other man, standing up and pointing to the photograph.

'In the mortuary at Épernay. Do you know her?'

The Englishman's face was inscrutable. But Maigret noticed that his huge, apoplectic neck had turned purple.

He picked up his white cap, put it on his bald head, and turning to his companion, muttered in English:

'More complications!'

Then, unconcerned by the interest being shown by the bargees, he puffed at his cigarette and stated:

'*C'est mon femme.*'

The pattering of the rain on the window-panes and even the creaking of the lock machinery could be heard much more clearly. The silence lasted a few seconds, completely unbroken, as if life had been suspended.

'You pay, Willy. . . .'

The Englishman threw his oilskins over his shoulders, without putting his arms in the sleeves, and growled at Maigret:

'Come on board. . . .'

The seaman he had called Vladimir finished off the bottle of champagne and then went out as he had come in, accompanied by Willy.

The first thing the Chief-Inspector saw when he arrived on board was a woman in a dressing-gown, her feet bare, her hair tousled, dozing on a red-velvet couch.

The Englishman touched her shoulder and with the same calm as before, in a tone of voice devoid of courtesy, said:

'Go outside.'

Then he waited, his eyes wandering over the folding table on which there was a bottle of whisky and half a dozen dirty glasses, as well as an ash-tray overflowing with cigarette ends.

He ended up by automatically pouring himself a drink

15

and pushed the bottle towards Maigret with a gesture which signified:

'If you want some . . .'

A barge went by on a level with the portholes and the carter fifty yards farther on stopped his horses, whose bells could be heard tinkling.

CHAPTER 2

The Southern Cross

MAIGRET was almost as tall and bulky as the Englishman. At the Quai des Orfèvres his sang-froid was a byword. Yet this time he was irritated by the other man's calm.

And that calm seemed to be the order of the day on board. From the seaman Vladimir to the woman who had just been roused from her sleep everyone had the same unconcerned or apathetic look. They were like people who had been dragged out of bed the morning after a tremendous binge.

One detail among a hundred. While she was getting up and looking for a packet of cigarettes, the woman caught sight of the photograph which the Englishman had placed on the table and which had got wet in the course of the brief journey from the Café de la Marine to the yacht.

'Mary?' she asked, with scarcely a start of surprise.

'Yes, it's Mary.'

And that was all. She went out through a door which opened forward and which presumably led to the bathroom.

Willy came on deck and went down in front of the hatchway. The saloon was tiny. The partitions of polished mahogany were extremely thin, and anyone forward could probably hear everything, for the owner looked that way first and then at the young man, saying with a certain impatience:

'Hurry up! Come in!'

And to Maigret he said curtly:

'Sir Walter Lampson, retired colonel of the Indian Army.'

He accompanied his own introduction with a stiff little bow and a wave towards the bench.

'And this gentleman?' asked the Chief-Inspector, turning to Willy.

17

'A friend of mine . . . Willy Marco. . . .'

'Spanish?'

The colonel shrugged his shoulders. Maigret looked hard at the young man's obviously Jewish features.

'Greek on my father's side . . . Hungarian on my mother's. . . .'

'I shall have to ask you a certain number of questions, Sir Walter. . . .'

Willy had perched nonchalantly on the back of a chair and was swaying to and fro while smoking a cigarette.

'I'm listening.'

But just as Maigret was going to begin, the yachtsman said in halting French:

'Who did it? Do you know?'

'We have no idea as yet. That is why you can help me considerably in my inquiries by clearing up certain points.'

'Rope?' the Englishman asked, touching his throat.

'No. The murderer used just his hands. When did you last see Mrs Lampson?'

'Willy . . .'

Willy was undeniably the general factotum, expected to do everything from ordering drinks to answering questions put to the colonel.

'At Meaux on Thursday evening,' he said.

'And you didn't inform the police that she had disappeared?'

'What for? She did as she pleased.'

'She often went off like that?'

'Sometimes.'

The rain was pattering on the deck above them. Dusk was giving place to night and Willy Marco turned on the electric light.

'Are the batteries charged?' the colonel asked him in English. 'It won't be like the other day, will it?'

Maigret was making an effort to give a definite direction to his interrogation. But he was constantly being distracted by new impressions.

In spite of himself he was looking at everything and thinking about everything at the same time, so that his head was full of a seething mass of shapeless ideas.

He was not so much outraged as embarrassed by this man who, in the Café de la Marine, had glanced at the photograph and stated without a tremor:

'*C'est mon femme.*'

He recalled the woman in the dressing-gown asking:

'Mary?'

And now Willy was swaying to and fro all the time, a cigarette between his lips, while the colonel was worrying about batteries!

In the neutral atmosphere of his office, the Chief-Inspector would probably have conducted an orderly interrogation. Here he began by taking his coat off without being asked, and picked up the photograph, which was as sinister as any other photograph of a corpse.

'You live in France?'

'France and England. . . . Sometimes Italy. . . . Always with my boat, the *Southern Cross.* . . .'

'Where have you come from?'

'Paris,' replied Willy, to whom the colonel had motioned to speak. 'We stayed there a fortnight, after spending a month in London.'

'You were living on board?'

'No. The boat was at Auteuil. We put up at the Hôtel Raspail, in Montparnasse. . . .'

'The colonel, his wife, the lady I saw just now, and yourself?'

'Yes. The lady is the widow of a Chilean politician, Madame Negretti.'

Sir Walter gave an impatient sigh and spoke again in English:

'Hurry up, or he'll still be here tomorrow morning. . . .'

Maigret did not bat an eyelid. But from then on he put his questions with a hint of brutality:

19

'Madame Negretti isn't a relation of yours, is she?' he asked Willy.

'No.'

'So she isn't connected in any way with you and the colonel. . . . Would you mind telling me how the cabins are arranged?'

'Forward there's the crew space where Vladimir sleeps. He was once a cadet in the Russian navy. He served in Wrangel's fleet. . . .'

'There are no other seamen? No servants?'

'Vladimir does everything. . . .'

'And then?'

'Between the crew space and this saloon, there's the galley on the right and the bathroom on the left.'

'And aft?'

'The engine.'

'So there were four of you in this cabin?'

'There are four bunks. . . . First of all the two benches you can see, which turn into divans . . . and then . . .'

Willy went over to one of the partitions and opened a sort of long drawer, revealing a complete bed.

'There's one on each side. . . . You see?'

Maigret was indeed beginning to see things a little more clearly and realized that it would not be very long before he had uncovered the secrets of this strange company.

The colonel's eyes were glazed and moist like those of a drunkard. He seemed to have lost interest in the conversation.

'What happened at Meaux? And first of all, when did you get there?'

'Wednesday evening. . . . Meaux is one day's journey from Paris. . . . We had brought along a couple of girls from Montparnasse. . . .'

'Go on.'

'It was a fine night. . . . We brought out the gramophone and danced on deck. . . . About four o'clock in the morning

I took our friends to the local hotel and they presumably caught a train back to Paris the next day.'

'Where was the *Southern Cross* moored?'

'Near the lock.'

'Did anything special happen on Thursday?'

'We got up very late, after being continually woken up by a crane loading stones into a barge next to us. . . . The colonel and I had an apéritif in town. . . . In the afternoon. . . wait a minute . . . the colonel had a nap . . . . I played chess with Gloria . . . Gloria is Madame Negretti. . . .'

'On deck?'

'I think Mary went out for a walk.'

'And she never came back?'

'Oh, yes! She had dinner on board. . . . The colonel suggested spending the evening in a dance-hall and Mary refused to come with us. . . . When we got back, about three in the morning, she wasn't here. . . .'

'You didn't make any inquiries?'

Sir Walter started drumming his fingers on the polished table.

'The colonel has already told you that his wife was free to come and go as she pleased. . . . We waited for her until Saturday and then we moved on. . . . She was familiar with the route we were taking and she knew where she could join us. . . .'

'You're on your way to the Mediterranean?'

'To the island of Porquerolles, opposite Hyères, where we spend the greater part of the year. . . . The colonel has bought an old fort there, the Petit Langoustier. . . .'

'Did everybody stay on board all day Friday?'

Willy hesitated, then replied rather hurriedly:

'I went to Paris. . . .'

'What for?'

He laughed, an unpleasant laugh which gave a peculiar twist to his mouth.

'I've already mentioned our two friends from Montparnasse . . . I wanted to see them again . . . one of them at least. . . .'

'Can you give me their names?'

'Their Christian names . . . . Suzy and Lia. . . . They're at the Coupole every night. . . . They live at the hotel on the corner of the rue de la Grande Chaumière. . . .'

'Professionals?'

'Sweet little things. . . .'

The door opened. Madame Negretti, who had put on a green silk dress, appeared in the doorway.

'May I come in?'

The colonel replied with a shrug of the shoulders. He must have been on his third whisky and he was drinking them with very little water.

'Willy . . . . ask about the formalities.'

Maigret did not need a translation to understand. This odd, casual way of asking him questions was beginning to get on his nerves.

'Naturally you will have to identify the body first of all. . . . After the post-mortem you will probably be able to obtain the burial permit. You choose the cemetery and . . .'

'Can we go straight away? Is there a garage where I can hire a motor?'

'At Épernay.'

'Willy . . . telephone for a motor . . . straight away. . . .'

'There's a telephone at the Café de la Marine,' said Maigret while the young man was grumpily putting on his oilskins.

'Where's Vladimir?'

'I heard him come back just now.'

'Tell him we're having dinner at Épernay. . . .'

Madame Negretti, who was a plump woman with shining black hair and pale flesh, had sat down in a corner, under the barometer, and was following the scene, her chin in her hand, with an absent-minded or deeply thoughtful expression.

'Are you coming with us?' Sir Walter asked her.

'I don't know.... Is it still raining?'

Maigret's nerves were on edge and the colonel's last question was not calculated to calm him down.

'How many days do you think we shall need for everything?'

He retorted fiercely:

'Including the funeral, I suppose?'

'Yes. . . . Three days?'

'If the police doctors issue the burial permit and if the examining magistrate doesn't oppose it, you could get it all over, materially speaking, within twenty-four hours. . . .'

Did the other man grasp the bitter irony of these words?

Maigret, for his part, felt the need to look at the photograph: a broken, dirty, crumpled body, a face which had once been pretty and powdered, with scented rouge on the lips and the cheeks, and whose grimace could not be looked at now without a shiver going down one's spine.

'Have a drink?'

'No, thanks.'

'Well, then . . .'

Sir Walter Lampson stood up to signify that he considered the conversation at an end, and called out:

'Vladimir! . . . a suit!'

'I shall probably have other questions to ask you,' said the Chief-Inspector. 'Perhaps I may have to search the yacht. . . .'

'Tomorrow . . . Épernay first, eh? . . . How long will it take by motor?'

'You're leaving me by myself?' Madame Negretti asked anxiously.

'With Vladimir. . . . You can come along if you like. . . .'

'I'm not dressed.'

Willy burst in and took off his dripping oilskins.

'The motor will be here in ten minutes. . . .'

'Then if you don't mind, Chief-Inspector . . .'

The colonel showed him the door.

'We have to dress . . .'

Maigret would have liked to punch somebody in the face as he left, he was so exasperated. He heard the hatchway shut behind him.

From outside, nothing could be seen but the light of eight portholes and the white lantern hooked on to the mast. Less than ten yards away the squat stern of a barge stood out in silhouette, and on the left, on the bank, a big pile of coal.

Perhaps it was an illusion. But Maigret had the impression that the rain was falling faster, that the sky was lower and darker than he had ever seen it.

He made for the Café de la Marine where the voices suddenly fell silent on his arrival. All the bargees were there, in a circle round the cast-iron stove. The lock-keeper was leaning on the bar, close to the daughter of the house, a tall, red-headed girl in clogs.

On the oilcloth on the tables there were bottles of wine, tumblers, puddles.

'Well, is it really his missus?' the proprietor asked at last, taking his courage in both hands.

'Yes. Give me a beer. No . . . something hot . . . toddy. . . .'

The bargees gradually started talking again. The girl brought the hot glass, brushing against Maigret's shoulder with her apron.

And the Chief-Inspector imagined the three people getting dressed in the narrow cabin, with Vladimir there as well.

He imagined a good many other things, but idly and not without a certain repugnance.

He knew the lock at Meaux, which was all the more important in that, like the one at Dizy, it formed a junction between the Marne and the canal, where there was a port in the shape of a half-moon, always crowded with barges packed tightly together.

There, in the midst of the barges, the *Southern Cross*

all lit up, with the two women from Montparnasse, fat Gloria Negretti, Mrs Lampson, Willy, and the colonel dancing on the deck to music from the gramophone, and drinking . . .

In a corner of the Café de la Marine, two men in blue overalls were eating sausages, which they were cutting with their pocket-knives as they went along, at the same time as their bread, and drinking red wine.

And somebody was describing an accident which had happened in the morning at the 'vault', in other words at the place where the canal, in order to cross the highest part of the Langres plateau, went underground for a distance of five miles.

A bargee had had his foot caught in the tow-rope; he had shouted without being able to make the carter hear him and, when the horses moved off after a rest, he had been thrown into the water.

There was no light in the tunnel. The barge carried only one lantern which cast only a faint gleam over the water. The bargee's brother—the boat was called *The Two Brothers* – had jumped into the canal.

Only one of them had been fished out, when he was already dead. They were still looking for the other. . . .

'They only had two annual instalments left to pay on their boat. But it seems that according to the contract their wives won't have to pay them. . . .'

A taxi-driver wearing a leather cap came in and looked round.

'Who ordered a motor here?'

'I did,' said Maigret.

'I've had to leave it at the bridge . . . I don't fancy diving into the canal. . . .'

'Are you eating here?' the proprietor asked the Chief-Inspector.

'I don't know.'

He went out with the taxi-driver. The white-painted *Southern Cross* made a milky patch in the rain and two boys from a near-by barge, oblivious of the downpour, were gazing at her in admiration.

'Joseph!' shouted a woman's voice. 'Bring your brother back . . . you're in for a hiding!'

'*Southern Cross*,' the taxi-driver read on the bows. 'They're English, are they?'

Maigret crossed the bridge and knocked. Willy, who was ready, very smart in a dark suit, opened the door, revealing the colonel, red-faced and in his shirt-sleeves, having his tie done by Gloria Negretti.

The cabin smelt of eau-de-Cologne and brilliantine.

'Has the motor arrived?' asked Willy. 'Is it here?'

'It's at the bridge, two miles away.'

Maigret stayed outside. He heard the colonel and the young man talking together in English. Finally Willy came out and said:

'He doesn't want to wade through the mud. Vladimir's going to lower the dinghy . . . we'll join you over there. . . .'

'Hmm!' muttered the taxi-driver, who had heard what he said.

Ten minutes later, he and Maigret were walking up and down on the stone bridge, beside the motor whose side-lights were burning. Nearly half an hour went by before they heard the throb of a little two-stroke engine.

Finally Willy's voice called out:

'Is it here? . . . Chief-Inspector!'

'Here, yes.'

The motor-boat described a circle and hove to. Vladimir helped the colonel on to the bank and agreed on a time for the return journey.

In the motor Sir Walter did not say a word. Despite his corpulence he was remarkably smart. Ruddy-faced, well groomed, and phlegmatic, he was very much the English gentleman as depicted in nineteenth-century prints.

Willy Marco smoked one cigarette after another.

'What a rattle-trap!' he sighed as the motor jolted over a gully.

Maigret noticed that he was wearing a platinum signet-ring with a big yellow diamond.

When they arrived in the town with its streets glistening with rain, the driver raised his window and asked:

'What's the address you want?'

'The mortuary!' replied the Chief-Inspector.

*

It did not take long. The colonel scarcely opened his lips. There was only one attendant in the building, where three bodies were stretched out on the slabs.

All the doors were already locked. The locks could be heard squeaking. A light had to be switched on.

It was Maigret who lifted the sheet.

'Yes.'

Willy was more upset, more impatient to get away.

'You recognize her too?'

'It's her all right. . . . As she is now . . . .'

He did not finish what he was saying. He was visibly turning pale. His lips were going dry. If the Chief-Inspector had not taken him outside he would probably have been sick.

'You don't know who did it?' said the colonel.

Perhaps it might have been possible to distinguish a scarcely perceptible tremor in his voice. But then that was probably the effect of all the whisky he had drunk.

All the same, Maigret made a mental note of that tiny weakening.

They found themselves outside on a pavement dimly lit by a street-lamp, opposite the motor whose driver had not left the wheel.

'You'll have dinner with us?' said Sir Walter, without even turning towards Maigret.

'No, thank you. I want to see to a few matters while I'm here.'

The colonel did not press him.

'Come along, Willy.'

Maigret remained for a moment in the doorway of the mortuary while the young man, after conferring with Sir Walter, bent forward to speak to the driver.

It was a question of finding out which was the best restaurant in the town. People went by, as well as clanking, brightly lit trams.

A few miles away lay the canal and, all the way along it, near the locks, sleeping barges which would move off at four o'clock in the morning, in a smell of stables and hot coffee.

CHAPTER 3

Mary's Necklace

WHEN Maigret had gone to bed, in a room whose characteristic smell caused him a certain queasiness, he spent some time comparing two pictures.

At Épernay first of all, seen through the brightly lit windows of the Bécasse, the best restaurant in the town, the colonel and Willy having dinner, surrounded by high-class waiters.

It was less than half an hour after the visit to the mortuary. Sir Walter Lampson was holding himself a little stiffly and the impassivity of his brick-red face, surmounted by a few silver hairs, was amazing.

Beside his elegance, or rather his breeding, Willy's, casual though it was, rang false.

Maigret had dined in another restaurant, and had telephoned first to the Prefecture and then to the Meaux police.

Then, all alone in the rainy night, he had walked along the long ribbon of the road. He had caught sight of the lighted portholes of the *Southern Cross* opposite the Café de la Marine.

And he had been inquisitive enough to go on board, under the pretext of a pipe he had left behind.

It was there that he had registered the second picture: In the mahogany cabin, still in his striped seaman's jersey and with a cigarette between his lips, Vladimir was sitting opposite Madame Negretti, whose oily hair was once again hanging down over her cheeks.

They were playing cards, a Central European game called Sixty-six.

There was a brief moment of amazement. But not even a start of surprise. Breaths were caught for a second. After

29

that Vladimir had got up to look for the pipe. Gloria Negretti had asked with a lisp:

'Aren't they back yet? . . . It really is Mary?'

The Chief-Inspector had felt like getting on his bicycle and following the canal so as to catch up with the barges which had spent the night between Sunday and Monday at Dizy. The sight of the soaking tow-path and the black sky had discouraged him.

When there was a knock on his door he realized, even before opening his eyes, that the grey light of dawn was filtering through the window into his room.

He had had a disturbed sleep, full of the stamping of horses, vague shouts, footsteps on the stairs, clinking glasses down below, and finally whiffs of coffee and hot rum which had come up to him.

'What is it?'

'Lucas. Can I come in?'

And Inspector Lucas, who nearly always worked with Maigret, pushed open the door and shook the moist hand which his chief held out to him through an opening in the sheets.

'Have you got something already? You're not too tired, old man?'

'Not really. Straight away after getting your phone call I went to the hotel in question, on the corner of the rue de la Grande Chaumière. The girls weren't there. I got their names in any case . . . *Suzanne Verdier, known as Suzy, born at Honfleur in 1906 . . . Lia Lauwenstein, born in the Grand Duchy of Luxemburg in 1903. . . .* The first arrived in Paris four years ago as a housemaid, then worked for some time as a model. . . . The Lauwenstein girl has lived mostly on the Riviera. Neither of them, I checked on that, is on the Vice Squad's lists . . . but they might just as well be.'

'Look, old man, would you mind passing me my pipe and ordering some coffee?'

Water could be heard splashing in the lock and a diesel engine running slowly. Maigret got out of bed and went across to a pitiful dressing-table where he poured some cold water into the bowl.

'Carry on. . . .'

'I went to the Coupole as you told me to. . . . They weren't there, but all the waiters know them. They sent me to the Dingo, then to the Cigogne. . . . Finally, in a little American bar whose name I've forgotten, in the rue Vavin, I found them by themselves, and not a bit stand-offish. . . . Lia isn't at all bad . . . she's got a style of her own. . . . Suzy is a sweet, harmless little blonde who would have made a good wife and mother if she'd stayed in her home-town . . . she's got freckles all over her face and . . .'

'You can't see a towel anywhere can you?' Maigret broke in, his face streaming with water and his eyes shut. 'Incidentally, is it still raining?'

'It wasn't raining when I arrived but it's going to start again any minute. At six o'clock this morning there was a fog that froze the air in your lungs. . . . Well, I offered the young ladies a drink. . . . They promptly asked for sand-wiches, which didn't surprise me to begin with . . . but after a while I noticed the string of pearls the Lauwenstein girl had got round her neck . . . . I bit on them by way of a joke. . . . They are absolutely genuine . . . not an American millionairess's necklace, but worth a hundred thousand all the same. . . . Well, when girls of that sort prefer chocolate and sandwiches to cocktails . . . .'

Maigret, who was smoking his first pipe of the day, went to open the door for the girl who had brought some coffee. Then he glanced out of the window at the yacht, where there was no sign of life as yet. A barge was passing the *Southern Cross*. The sailor at the wheel was looking at his neighbour with grudging admiration.

'Right . . . go on. . . .'

'I took them somewhere else, to a quiet café. . . . There I suddenly showed them my badge, then pointed to the necklace and said on the off-chance:

'"Those are Mary Lampson's pearls, aren't they?"

'The two of them probably didn't know that she was dead. In any case, if they did know, they played their parts perfectly.

'It took them a few minutes before they opened up. It was Suzy in the end who told the other girl:

'"You'd better tell him the truth, seeing that he knows so much already."

'And it was quite a story.... Do you want a hand, chief?'

Maigret was in fact trying in vain to catch hold of the braces which were hanging down his thighs.

'The most important point first: they both swore that it was Mary Lampson herself who gave them the pearls last Friday in Paris, where she came to see them.... You probably understand better than I do, because I know nothing about the case except what you told me over the phone....

'I asked if Willy Marco was with Mrs Lampson. They say not, and maintain that they haven't seen Willy since Thursday, when they left him at Meaux ...'

'Hold on a minute!' said Maigret, knotting his tie in front of a greyish mirror which deformed his reflection. 'On Wednesday evening the *Southern Cross* arrives at Meaux.... Our two young things are on board.... They have a gay time that night with the colonel, Willy, Mary Lampson, and the Negretti woman....

'Late at night Suzy and Lia are taken to a hotel and they leave by train on Thursday morning.... Were they given any money?'

'Five hundred francs, they say.'

'They met the colonel in Paris?'

'A few days earlier....'

'And what happened on board the yacht?'

Lucas gave a peculiar smile.

'Some not very pretty fun and games.... It seems that the Englishman lives for nothing but whisky and women ... Madame Negretti is his mistress....'

'Did his wife know?'

'Oh, yes! She herself was Willy's mistress. . . . Not that that prevented them from taking Suzies and Lias along with them. . . . You cotton on? . . . And on top of that, Vladimir danced with all the women. . . . At dawn there was a quarrel because Lia Lauwenstein complained that five hundred francs was just a tip. . . . The colonel didn't even answer them, leaving that to Willy. . . . Everybody was drunk. . . . The Negretti woman was asleep on the roof and Vladimir had to carry her into the cabin. . . .'

Standing at the window, Maigret let his gaze wander along the dark line of the canal and on the left he could see the little Decauville train still carting earth and rubble around.

The sky was grey, with, lower down, scraps of black clouds, but it was not raining.

'Go on. . . .'

'That's about all. . . . On Friday Mary Lampson is supposed to have gone to Paris where she met our two young ladies and gave them her necklace. . . .'

'Well, well! Just a little token gift!'

'Oh, no! She gave it to them to sell it and give her half the price they got for it. . . . She told them that her husband never let her have any ready money. . . .'

The wallpaper of the room had a pattern of little yellow flowers. The enamel jug added a pale note to the scene.

Maigret saw the lock-keeper hurrying along with a bargee and his carter to drink a glass of rum at the bar.

'That's all I got out of them,' concluded Lucas. 'I left them at two in the morning, telling Inspector Dufour to keep a discreet eye on them. Then I went to the Prefecture to go through the files, in accordance with your instructions. I found a card on Willy Marco, who was expelled from Monaco four years ago after a rather obscure gambling affair, and held at Nice the following year on a complaint by an American woman who had been relieved of a few jewels. But the complaint was withdrawn, I don't know why, and Marco allowed to go free. You think it was he who . . .?'

'I don't think anything. And I swear that I mean that. Don't forget that the murder was committed on Sunday after ten o'clock at night, when the *Southern Cross* was moored at La Ferté-sous-Jouarre. . . .'

'What do you think of the colonel?'

Maigret shrugged his shoulders and pointed to Vladimir, who had climbed out of the forward hatchway and was coming towards the Café de la Marine, dressed in white trousers, canvas shoes, and a sweater, with an American beret over one ear.

'Somebody wants Monsieur Maigret on the telephone,' the red-headed girl shouted from behind the door.

'Come downstairs with me, old man. . . .'

The telephone was in the corridor, next to a coat stand.

'Hullo . . . is that Meaux? What's that you said? . . . Yes, the *Providence*. . . . She spent all day Thursday taking on cargo at Meaux? . . . Left on Friday at three in the morning. . . . No others? . . . The *Éco III*. . . . She's a tanker, isn't she? . . . Friday night at Meaux . . . left Saturday morning. . . . Thank you, Chief-Inspector. . . . Yes, ask questions as you think fit . . . I'm still at the same address!'

Lucas had listened to this conversation without understanding it. Before Maigret had time to open his mouth to explain, a police cyclist appeared at the door.

'An urgent message from Police Headquarters!'

The policeman had mudstains up to his belt.

'Go and dry yourself and drink my health in a hot toddy. . . .'

Maigret took the inspector out on to the tow-path, opened the envelope, and read in an undertone:

'*Summary of the first analyses made in connexion with the Dizy case: many traces of resin found in the victim's hair as well as chestnut-coloured horse-hairs. . . . The stomach, at the time death occurred, contained some red wine and some preserved beef of the type sold under the name of corned beef.*'

'Eight horses out of ten have got chestnut hair!' sighed Maigret.

*

Vladimir, in the shop, was asking about the nearest place where he could do his shopping and there were three people advising him, including the police cyclist from Épernay, who finally went off with the seaman in the direction of the stone bridge.

Maigret, followed by Lucas, made for the stable where, the previous evening, the proprietor's grey horse had been joined by a broken-kneed mare that there was talk of killing.

'She can't have picked up the resin here,' remarked the Chief-Inspector.

He followed the path from the canal to the stable twice over, going round the buildings.

'Do you sell resin?' he asked, catching sight of the proprietor pushing a wheelbarrow full of potatoes.

'Well, it isn't really resin. . . . We call it Norwegian tar. . . . They use it on the wooden barges above the water-line. . . . Farther down they make do with coal-tar, which is twenty times cheaper. . . .'

'Have you got any in stock?'

'There's always a couple of dozen cans in the shop . . . but we don't sell any in this weather. . . . The bargees wait for the sun before doing up their boats. . . .'

'Is the *Éco III* made of wood?'

'No, iron like most motor-barges.'

'And the *Providence*?'

'Wood . . . Have you found anything?'

Maigret did not reply.

'You know what they're saying?' continued the man, who had put down his wheelbarrow.

'Who are *they*?'

'The canal folk, the bargees, the pilots, the lock-keepers. A motor-car would have a job to go along the tow-path . . . but what about a motor-bike? And a motor-bike can go a long way, without leaving much more trace than a push-bike. . . .'

The door of the cabin of the *Southern Cross* opened. But nobody could be seen yet.

For a moment one point in the sky turned a yellowish colour, as if the sun were at last going to break through. Maigret and Lucas paced silently up and down beside the canal.

Before five minutes had gone by the wind was bending the reeds and a minute later the rain was pouring down.

Maigret held out his hand in a mechanical gesture. In a gesture no less mechanical, Lucas took a packet of grey tobacco out of his pocket and handed it to his companion.

They stopped for a moment in front of the lock, which was empty and being made ready, for an invisible tug had hooted three times in the distance, which meant that she was towing three boats.

'Where do you think the *Providence* is now?' Maigret asked the lock-keeper.

'Wait a minute . . . Mareuil . . . Condé . . . near Aigny there are a dozen barges in a row and they'll slow her up. . . . The lock at Vraux has only got two of its sluices work-ing. . . . I'd say she's at Saint-Martin. . . .'

'Is that far from here?'

'Just twenty miles.'

'And the *Éco III*?'

'She ought to be at La Chaussée . . . but a fellow going downstream told me last night that she'd broken her pro-peller at Lock 12 . . . so that you'll find her at Tours-sur-Marne, ten miles from here. . . . They've only themselves to blame. . . . The regulations forbid them to carry a load of two hundred and eighty tons, and they all insist on doing it. . . .'

*

It was ten o'clock in the morning. When Maigret got on the bicycle he had hired, he caught sight of the colonel sitting in a rocking-chair on the deck of the yacht and opening the Paris newspapers which the postman had just delivered.

'Nothing special!' he said to Lucas. 'Stay around here ... don't let them too much out of your sight. ...'

The rain thinned out. The road was straight. At the third lock the sun appeared, still a little pale, making the raindrops glisten on the reeds.

From time to time Maigret had to get off his bicycle to pass a barge's horses which, harnessed together, took up the whole width of the tow-path, moving one leg after another, in an effort which threw every muscle into relief.

Two horses were being led by a little girl between eight and ten, wearing a red dress and carrying her doll at arm's length.

The villages, for the most part, were at a fair distance from the canal. The result was that that regular ribbon of still water seemed to stretch away in absolute solitude.

A field here and there, with men bent over the dark earth. But nearly always woods. And reeds five or six foot high added still further to the impression of calm.

A barge was taking on a load of chalk near a quarry, in a cloud of dust which was whitening her hull and the men working on her.

In the lock at Saint-Martin there was a boat sure enough, but it was not the *Providence*.

'They must be having dinner in the reach above Châlons,' said the lock-keeper's wife, who was coming and going from one lock to the other, followed by two children clinging to her skirts.

Maigret had a stubborn nature. He was surprised, about eleven o'clock, to find himself in a spring-like setting, an atmosphere vibrating with sunshine and warmth.

In front of him, the canal stretched away in a straight line for five miles, lined on both sides by fir-woods.

Right at the end, one could just make out the

light-coloured walls of a lock whose gates were oozing trickles of water.

Half-way along, a barge was stationary, a little askew. Her two horses had been unharnessed and each with its head buried in a bag, were eating oats and stretching themselves.

The first impression was gay or at least restful. There was not a house in sight. And the gleams of light on the calm water were broad and slow.

A little more pedalling, and at the stern of the barge the Chief-Inspector could see a table laid underneath the awning protecting the tiller. The oilcloth was a blue-and-white check. A fair-haired woman was putting down a steaming dish in the middle.

He got off his bicycle after reading the name *Providence* on the round, shining hull.

One of the horses looked hard at him, moved its ears, and gave a peculiar moan before beginning to eat again.

*

Between the barge and the bank there was only a thin, narrow plank which bent under Maigret's weight. Two men were eating, following him with their eyes, while the woman came to meet him.

'What do you want?' she asked, buttoning her half-open blouse over a buxom bosom.

Her accent was almost as musical as that of the south of France. She was not in the least uneasy. She waited. She seemed to be protecting the two men with her joyous corpulence.

'Some information,' said the Chief-Inspector. 'You probably know that a murder has been committed at Dizy. . . .'

'The people on the *Castor et Pollux*, which passed us this morning, told us about it. . . . Is it true? . . . It's almost impossible, isn't it? . . . How could anybody have done it? . . . And on the canal, where everybody's so quiet!'

Her cheeks were blotchy. The two men went on eating,

38

without taking their eyes off Maigret. The latter automatically glanced at the dish which was full of a dark-coloured meat with a smell which puzzled him.

'A kid I bought this morning at Aigny Lock. . . . You wanted to ask us for some information? . . . But we'd gone before they found the corpse. . . . Incidentally, have they found out who the poor lady was?'

One of the two men was short and dark, with a drooping moustache and something gentle and docile about him.

He was the husband. He had simply given the intruder a casual nod, leaving his wife to do the talking.

The other man was probably about sixty. His hair, extremely thick and badly cut, was white. An inch or two of beard covered his chin and the greater part of his cheeks, so that, what with his thick eyebrows, he looked as hairy as an animal.

In contrast his eyes were bright and expressionless.

'It's your carter that I'd like to ask a few questions. . . .'

The woman laughed.

'Jean? . . . I'd better warn you that he doesn't talk much. . . . He's our bear! . . . Just look at him eating. . . . But he's the best carter you could find. . . .'

The old man's fork had stopped moving. He was looking at Maigret with curiously limpid eyes.

Certain village idiots have that sort of look in their eyes, and also certain animals used to gentle treatment when they are suddenly treated roughly.

A dazed expression. But something else too, something indescribable, a sort of withdrawing into one's shell.

'What time did you get up to see to your horses?'

'Usual time. . . .'

He had shoulders of a breadth which was all the more astonishing in that he had very short legs.

'Jean gets up every morning at half past two,' the woman broke in. 'Just look at our horses . . . they're groomed like race-horses every day . . . and at night you'll never get him to have a drink before he's rubbed the horses down. . . .'

39

'Do you sleep in the stable?'

Jean looked as though he did not understand. Once again it was the woman who pointed to a taller construction in the middle of the boat.

'That's the stable,' she said. 'He always sleeps there. We've got our cabin aft. Do you want to see it?'

The deck was spotlessly clean, the brasses more highly polished than on the *Southern Cross*. And when the woman opened a pair of doors in deal, with a stained-glass skylight over them, Maigret saw a touching little saloon.

There was the same fake antique furniture in oak as in the most traditional of lower-middle-class homes. The table was covered with a cloth embroidered with silks of different colours and held vases, framed photographs, and a flower-stand overflowing with green plants.

There were more embroidered cloths on a sideboard. The arm-chairs were protected by net covers.

'If Jean had wanted, we'd have fixed up a bed for him near us . . . but he says he can't sleep anywhere except in the stable . . . even though we're always afraid of him get-ting kicked one day. . . . It's all right him saying the horses know him. . . . When they're asleep . . . .'

She had started eating, the typical housewife cooking for others who picks the worst food for herself without even thinking about it.

Jean had stood up and kept looking, now at his horses, now at the Chief-Inspector, while the skipper was rolling a cigarette.

'And you didn't see anything or hear anything?' Maigret asked, gazing hard at the carter.

The man turned towards the skipper's wife who an-swered him with her mouth full:

'You can be sure that if he'd seen anything he'd have said so.'

'The *Marie*'s arriving!' her husband announced anxiously.

For a few moments the air had been filled with the throbbing of an engine. Now the silhouette of a barge could be seen behind the *Providence*.

Jean looked at the woman, who looked hesitantly at Maigret.

'Look,' she said in the end. 'If you've got to talk to Jean, would you mind doing it on the move? . . . In spite of her engine, the *Marie* goes slower than we do. . . . If she gets in front of us before the lock, she'll block our way for three days. . . .'

Jean had not waited for these last sentences. He had removed the bags of oats from the heads of his horses, which he was leading a hundred yards in front of the barge.

The skipper picked up a tin trumpet and blew a shaky blast on it.

'Are you staying on board? . . . We'll tell you all we know, you understand. . . . Everybody knows us on the canals, from Liège to Lyons. . . .'

'I'll join you at the lock,' said Maigret, who had left his bicycle on the bank.

The gangway was removed. A figure had just appeared on the lock gates and the sluices were being opened. The horses moved off to an accompaniment of bells, waving the red pompons they wore on their heads.

Jean walked along beside them, slow, indifferent.

And the motor-barge, two hundred yards behind, slowed down on seeing that she had arrived too late.

Maigret followed, holding the handlebar of his bicycle with one hand. He could see the woman hurriedly finishing her meal, and her husband, a tiny, thin, inconsistent figure, practically lying over a tiller which was too heavy for him.

CHAPTER 4

The Lover

'I'VE had my lunch!' announced Maigret, coming into the Café de la Marine where Lucas was sitting by a window.

'At Aigny?' asked the proprietor. 'It's my brother-in-law who keeps the inn there. . . .'

'Bring us some beer.'

It was like a wager. The Chief-Inspector, toiling away on his bicycle, had scarcely come within sight of Dizy before the weather had clouded over. And now raindrops were slashing the last ray of sunshine.

The *Southern Cross* was still in her place. There was nobody to be seen on deck. And there was no sound coming from the lock, so that for the first time Maigret had the impression of being in the country on hearing the hens clucking in the yard.

'Nothing new?' he asked the inspector.

'The seaman came back with his shopping. The woman appeared for a moment, wearing a blue dressing-gown. The colonel and Willy came in here for an apéritif. They gave me a suspicious look, I think. . . .'

Maigret took the tobacco his companion offered him and filled his pipe while he waited for the proprietor who had served them to disappear into his shop.

'I've got no news either,' he growled. 'Of the two boats which could have brought Mary Lampson, one has broken down ten miles from here and the other is creeping along the canal at two miles an hour. . . .

'The first is made of iron . . . so it's impossible for the corpse to have picked up any resin on it. . . .

'The second is a wooden boat. The bargee's name is Canelle. . . . A nice motherly body who insisted on making me drink a glass of horrible rum, and a tiny husband running round her like a spaniel.

'The only person you could possibly suspect is their carter. . . . Either he's playing dumb, and in that case he's an amazingly good actor, or else he's a stupid brute. . . . He's been with them for eight years. . . . If the husband's a spaniel this fellow Jean's a bulldog. . . .

'He gets up at half past two in the morning, sees to his horses, gulps down a bowl of coffee, and starts walking along beside the animals. . . .

'Like that he pulls the barge along twenty or twenty-five miles a day, at the same steady pace, with a glass of white wine at every lock. . . .

'In the evening he rubs the horses down, has supper without saying a word, and drops on to his bale of straw, usually fully dressed. . .

'I've seen his papers: an old military pay-book in which you can scarcely turn the pages, they're so filthy. His name is Jean Liberge, and he was born at Lille in 1869.

'That's all . . . or rather, no . . . you'd have to assume that Mary Lampson was taken on board on Thursday evening, at Meaux. . . . Well, she was alive then . . . and she was still alive when she arrived here on Sunday evening. . . .

'It's physically impossible to hide a human being two days against her will in the stable on that boat . . .

'So that all three of them would have to be guilty. . . .'

And Maigret's grimace showed that he did not believe this.

'As for the idea that the victim went on board of her own free will. . . . You know what you're going to do, old man? Ask Sir Walter for his wife's maiden name . . . get on the phone and find out all you can about her. . . .'

There were still some rays of sunshine in two or three places in the sky, but the rain was falling more and more heavily. Lucas had scarcely left the Café de la Marine, making for the yacht, before Willy Marco came down the gangway, a loose-limbed, nonchalant figure in town clothes, with a vacant look in his eyes.

It was definitely a common feature of the entire company of the *Southern Cross* to look all the time like people who have not had enough sleep or who are suffering from a hang-over.

The two men passed each other on the tow-path. Willy appeared to hesitate when he saw the inspector go on board, then, lighting another cigarette from the one he had just finished smoking, he made straight for the café.

It was Maigret he was looking for, without attempting to disguise the fact.

He did not take off his soft hat, which he touched casually with one finger, murmuring:

'Good morning, Chief-Inspector. . . . Slept well? . . . I'd like to have a word with you. . . .'

'Fire away. . . .'

'Not here, if you don't mind. . . . We couldn't go up to your room, for instance, could we?'

He had lost nothing of his nonchalance. His little eyes were sparkling with what was almost an expression of mischievous pleasure.

'Cigarette?'

'No, thank you.'

'I was forgetting you were a pipe-smoker. . . .'

Maigret decided to take him up to his room, which had not yet been cleaned. Straight away, after a glance at the yacht, Willy sat down on the edge of the bed and began:

'Naturally you've already checked on my record. . . .'

He looked round for an ash-tray, failed to find one, and dropped his ash on the floor.

'Not so good, is it? . . . Not that I've ever tried to pass myself off as a little saint. . . . And the colonel tells me three times a day that I'm a skunk. . . .'

What was extraordinary was the frank expression on his

44

face. Maigret even admitted to himself that after making an unpleasant impression on him at first, the man now struck him as quite tolerable.

A peculiar mixture. Craftiness, cunning. But at the same time a spark of decency which redeemed the rest, and a hint of roguishness too, which was disarming.

'Mind you, I was educated at Eton, like the Prince of Wales. . . . If we were the same age, we'd probably be the best of friends . . . only my father is a fig-merchant at Smyrna . . . and I can't bear that sort of thing! . . . I got into one or two scrapes. . . . The mother of one of my friends at Eton helped me for a while. . . . You don't mind if I don't tell you her name, do you? . . . . A charming woman . . . but her husband became a Cabinet minister and she was afraid of compromising him. . . .

'After that . . . You must have heard about Monaco and then the business at Nice. . . . The truth isn't really as ugly as that . . . let me give you a piece of advice: never believe anything you're told by a middle-aged American woman who spends her time having fun on the Riviera and whose husband arrives without warning from Chicago. . . . Stolen jewels aren't always stolen . . . but let's forget about that. . . .

'Now about the necklace. . . . Either you know already or you haven't found out yet. . . . I'd have liked to talk to you about it last night, but in view of the circumstances it probably wouldn't have been decent. . . .

'The colonel is a gentleman after all. . . . Admittedly he's a bit too fond of his whisky . . . but that isn't surprising. . . . He ought to have ended up as a general and he was one of the coming men in Delhi when on account of a woman – she was the daughter of an important Indian personage – he was put on the retired list. . . .

'You've seen him yourself . . . . a splendid man, with tremendous appetites. . . . Out there, he had thirty boys, orderlies, secretaries, and heaven knows how many motors and horses at his disposal . . . and then, all of a sudden, nothing: something like a hundred thousand francs a year . . . .

'Did I tell you that he'd already been married twice before meeting Mary? . . . His first wife died in India. . . . The second time he divorced, taking all the blame on himself, after finding his wife with a boy. . . . A real gentleman! . . .'

And Willy, leaning back on the bed, swung one leg slowly to and fro, while Maigret, his pipe between his teeth, stood motionless with his back to the wall.

'And there you are. . . . Nowadays he spends his time as best he can. . . . At Porquerolles he lives in his old fort, the Petit Langoustier. . . . When he's saved enough money he goes to Paris or London. . . . But just think that in India he used to give a dinner every week to thirty or forty guests. . . .'

'Was it about the colonel that you wanted to speak to me?' murmured Maigret.

Willy did not bat an eyelid.

'The fact is, I was trying to put you in the picture . . . seeing that you've never lived in India or in London, and never had thirty boys and heaven knows how many pretty girls at your disposal. . . . I'm not trying to annoy you . . .

'To cut a long story short, I met him two years ago. . . . You didn't know Mary when she was alive. . . . A charming woman but with a bird-brain. . . . A bit hysterical too. . . . If people weren't fussing over her all the time she'd throw a fit or start a scene. . . .

'Do you know how old the colonel is? . . . Sixty-eight. . . . She made him tired, you understand? . . . Admittedly she let him play around – because he still likes his little bit of fun – but she was a bit of a nuisance. . . . She fell for me . . . I was quite fond of her. . . .'

'I suppose that Madame Negretti is Sir Walter's mistress?'

'Yes,' admitted the young man, pulling a face. 'It's hard to explain to you. . . . He can't live or drink on his own. . . . He needs people around him. . . . We met her one day when

46

we'd put in at Bandol. . . . The next morning she didn't go. . . . For him, that's enough! . . . She'll stay as long as she likes. . . .

'With me, it's a different matter . . . I'm one of the few men who can hold whisky as well as the colonel . . . except perhaps Vladimir, whom you've seen, and who puts us in our bunks nine times out of ten. . . .

'I don't know if you really understand my position. . . . Admittedly I don't have to worry about money . . . even though we sometimes stay a fortnight in a port waiting for a cheque from London to be able to buy some petrol!

'Why, the necklace I was talking about just now has been to the pawnshop a score of times. . . . Still, we don't often run out of whisky. . . . It isn't a life of luxury . . . but we sleep as long as we like . . . we come and go. . . . For my part, I prefer this to my father's figs. . . .

'In the beginning, the colonel had given his wife a few jewels. . . . She would ask him for some money now and then . . . for her clothes, you know, and to have a little ready cash. . . .

'Whatever you think, I swear it was a real shock for me yesterday to see that it was Mary in that awful photo. . . . For the colonel too, for that matter! . . . But he'd rather be torn to pieces than show it. . . . That's how he is! A real Englishman!

'When we left Paris last week – it's Tuesday today, isn't it? – the exchequer was very low. . . . The colonel wired to London to ask for an advance on his pension. . . . We were waiting for it at Épernay. . . . The money-order may have arrived by now. . . .

'The trouble was, I'd left a few debts in Paris. . . . Two or three times already, I'd ask Mary why she didn't sell her necklace. . . . She could have told her husband that she'd lost it, or that it had been stolen. . . .

'On Thursday night there was the little party you know about. . . . You mustn't get any wrong ideas about it. . . . As soon as Lampson sees some pretty girls, he's got to invite them on board . . . then, a couple of hours later, once he's tight, he gives me the job of getting rid of them as cheaply as possible.

'On Thursday, Mary was up much earlier than usual, and when we got out of our bunks she was already outside. . . .

'After lunch we stayed alone together for a little while, she and I. . . . She was very affectionate, in a strange rather sad sort of way. . . .

'At one point she put her necklace in my hand and said: '"You'll be able to sell it. . . ."

'I don't care if you don't believe me . . . . I was a bit embarrassed, a bit upset. . . . If you'd known her, you'd understand. . . . Just as she could be unpleasant sometimes, at other times she could be very touching. . . .

'You wouldn't understand. . . . She was forty years old. . . . She did her best to keep her end up . . . but she must have felt that she was finished. . . .

'Somebody came in . . . I put the necklace in my pocket. . . . In the evening the colonel took us to the dance-hall and Mary stayed behind. . . .

'When we got back, she wasn't there. . . . Lampson didn't worry, because it wasn't the first time she'd gone off like that. . . .

'And not on the spree, either. . . . Once, for instance, during the Porquerolles festival, there was a regular orgy at the Petit Langoustier that went on for nearly a week. . . .

'The first day or two, Mary was the liveliest of us all. . . . The third day she disappeared . . . and do you know where we found her? In an inn at Grien, where she was spending her time mothering two filthy little kids. . . .

'The business of the necklace worried me. . . . On Friday I went to Paris. . . . I nearly sold it. . . . Then I told myself that if there were any complications, I might get into trouble. . . .

'I thought of the two girls who'd been with us the day before. . . . You can do what you like with those kids. . . .

Besides, I'd already met Lia at Nice and I knew I could count on her.

'I left the necklace with her . . . just in case, I told her, if anyone asked her, to say that Mary had given it to her herself to sell. . . .

'It's as simple as that. . . . Stupid, really . . . I'd have done better to keep quiet. . . . The fact remains that unless I happen on some intelligent coppers, it's the sort of thing to land me in the Assize Court. . . .

'I realized that yesterday when I heard that Mary had been strangled. . . .

'I'm not asking what you think . . . indeed, to be perfectly frank, I quite expect to be arrested. . . .

'That would be a mistake, that's all . . . but if you want me to help you, I'm ready to give you a hand. . . . There are several things which may strike you as peculiar and which are really very simple. . . .'

He was practically lying on the bed and still smoking, his eyes fixed on the ceiling.

Maigret went and planted himself in front of the window to hide his perplexity.

'Does the colonel know about your coming to see me?' he asked, swinging round suddenly.

'No more than he knows about the business of the necklace . . . and . . . I'm in no position to make conditions, I realize that . . . but I'd rather he went on knowing nothing about it. . . .'

'Madame Negretti?'

'A dead weight! A pretty woman incapable of anything but lying on a divan, smoking cigarettes, and drinking liqueurs. . . . She started the day she arrived on board, and she's never stopped. . . . Oh, I beg your pardon! She plays cards too . . . indeed, I think it's her only passion. . . .'

The screech of rusty iron announced that the lock gates were being opened. . . . . Two donkeys went past the house and stopped a little farther on, while an empty barge went gliding along on its course as if it wanted to climb the bank.

Vladimir, bent double, was baling out the rain-water collecting in the dinghy.

A motor-car crossed the stone bridge, tried to drive on to the tow-path, braked, carried out a few clumsy manœuvres, and finally came to a complete stop.

A man in black got out. Willy, who had stood up, glanced out of the window and said:

'The undertaker.'

'When does the colonel expect to move on?'

'Straight after the funeral.'

'And that will take place here?'

'Why not? He's already got one wife buried near Delhi, and another married to a New-Yorker who'll end up under American soil. . . .'

Maigret glanced at him in spite of himself, to see if he was joking. But Willy Marco looked perfectly serious, except for that ambiguous little gleam in his eyes.

'Let's hope the money-order has arrived! . . . Otherwise the funeral will have to wait. . . .'

The man in black hesitated in front of the yacht, spoke to Vladimir who answered him without interrupting his work, and finally went on board, where he disappeared into the cabin.

Maigret had seen nothing more of Lucas.

'Off you go!' he said.

Willy hesitated. An anxious expression passed fleetingly over his features.

'Are you going to speak to him about the necklace?'

'I don't know. . . .'

It was finished already. Carefree once more, Willy connected the fold in his soft hat, gave a wave of the hand, and went downstairs.

When Maigret went down in his turn, there were two bargees at the bar, each with a mug of beer.

'Your friend's on the phone,' the proprietor told him. 'He asked for Moulins.'

A tug hooted in the distance. Maigret automatically counted the hoots and muttered under his breath:

'Five.'

That was canal life. Five barges arriving. The lock-keeper, wearing clogs, came out of his house and made for his sluices.

Lucas came back from the telephone with his face red.

'Whew! . . . That was a job!'

'What is it?'

'The colonel told me that his wife's maiden name was Marie Dupin. . . . For the marriage ceremony she produced a birth-certificate in that name, issued at Moulins. . . . I've just phoned there, saying it was a priority call. . . .'

'Well?'

'There's only one Marie Dupin registered at Moulins. She's forty-two, has three children, and is married to a certain Piedbœuf who's a baker in the rue Haute. . . . The Town Clerk who answered me saw her only yesterday behind her counter and it seems she weighs all of thirteen stone. . . .'

Maigret said nothing. Like a gentleman of leisure with nothing to do, he went over to the lock without bothering about his companion, and watched the whole operation. But every now and then he thrust his thumb furiously into the bowl of his pipe.

A little later Vladimir came up to the lock-keeper, and after touching his white cap, asked where he could fill up with drinking-water.

CHAPTER 5

The Y.C.F. Badge

MAIGRET had gone to bed early, while Lucas, to whom he had given his instructions, had set off for Meaux, Paris, and Moulins.

When he had left the bar-room there were three people drinking there, a couple of bargees and the wife of one of them, who had come to join her husband and was knitting in a corner.

It was gloomy and close. Outside, a barge had moored less than six feet from the *Southern Cross*, whose portholes were all lit up.

All of a sudden the Chief-Inspector was roused from a dream so vague that he could remember nothing about it as he opened his eyes. Somebody was hammering on his door while a frantic voice was shouting.

'Chief-Inspector! . . . Chief-Inspector! . . . Quick! . . . My father . . .'

Still in his pyjamas, he ran to open the door and the next moment the innkeeper's daughter hurled herself upon him in an unexpected frenzy, literally throwing herself into his arms.

'There! . . . Hurry. . . . No, stay . . . I don't dare to stay here alone . . . I don't want to . . . I'm frightened. . . .'

He had never paid much attention to her. He had regarded her as a solid, well-built girl without any nerves.

And here she was, her face ravaged, her body heaving, clinging to him with embarrassing fervour. Trying to free himself, he went over to the window and threw it open.

It must have been six o'clock in the morning. Day was just breaking, as cold as a winter dawn.

A hundred yards from the *Southern Cross*, in the direction

of the stone bridge and the Épernay road, four or five men were trying to get hold of something floating in the water, with the aid of a heavy boat-hook, while a bargee had untied his punt and was beginning to row.

Maigret was dressed in crumpled pyjamas. He threw his overcoat over his shoulders and looked for his shoes, which he put straight on his bare feet.

'You know! . . . It's *him*. . . . They've . . .'

With an abrupt movement he freed himself from the strange girl's embrace, went downstairs, and arrived outside just as a woman carrying a baby was approaching the group.

He had not been present when Mary Lampson's body had been discovered. But this new find was perhaps even more sinister, for with another crime an almost supernatural anguish hung over this stretch of the canal.

The men kept calling out to each other. The proprietor of the Café de la Marine, who had been the first to see a human body floating in the water, was directing their efforts.

Twice the boat-hook had touched the corpse. But the hook had slipped. The body had gone a few inches under the water before coming to the surface again.

Maigret had already recognized Willy's dark suit. He could not see the face because the head, being heavier, was submerged.

The bargee in the punt suddenly bumped into it, grabbed the dead man by the chest, and hauled him out of the water with one hand. But then he had to be dragged over the side of the boat.

The man had no feelings. He lifted the legs one after the other, threw his mooring-rope ashore, and wiped his streaming forehead with the back of his hand.

For a brief moment Maigret caught sight of Vladimir's sleepy head emerging from the hatchway on the yacht. The Russian rubbed his eyes. Then he disappeared.

'Don't touch anything.'

A bargee behind him protested, muttering that his

brother-in-law, in Alsace, had been brought back to life
after spending nearly three hours in the water.

The café proprietor for his part, pointed to the corpse's
throat. There, clearly visible, were two black finger-marks,
like those on Mary Lampson's neck.

This tragedy was the more disturbing of the two. Willy's
eyes were wide open, even bigger than usual. His right
hand was clutching a fistful of reeds.

Maigret had the impression of an unusual presence behind
him, and turned round to find the colonel standing there,
likewise in pyjamas, with a silk dressing-gown over them
and blue kid slippers on his feet.

His silver hair was tousled, his face a little puffy. And it
was odd to see him there, dressed like that, among the
bargees in their clogs and rough clothes, in the damp,
muddy dawn.

He was the tallest and broadest of them all. He gave off
a vague smell of eau-de-Cologne.

'It's Willy!' he said in a hoarse voice.

Then he said a few words in English, too fast for Maigret
to understand, bent down, and touched the young man's
face.

The girl who had woken the Chief-Inspector was leaning
against the door of the café, sobbing. The lock-keeper came
running up.

'Telephone the police at Épernay. . . . A doctor. . . .'

The Negretti woman herself appeared barefoot and dishevelled, but did not dare to leave the deck of the yacht,
and called to the colonel:

'Walter! . . . Walter!'

In the background there were people nobody had seen
arrive: the driver of the little train, some navvies, and a
peasant whose cow went on following the tow-path by
herself.

'Carry him into the café . . . touching him as little as
possible.'

There could be no doubt that he was dead. The smart

suit, which was now nothing but a rag, trailed on the ground while they were lifting the body.

The colonel followed slowly and his dressing-gown, his blue slippers, and his brick-coloured head on which a few long hairs were stirring in the wind made him look at once ridiculous and hieratical.

The girl started sobbing louder than ever when the corpse passed near her, and ran to shut herself up in the kitchen. The proprietor was yelling into the telephone:

'No, Mademoiselle! . . . The police! . . . Hurry! . . . It's a murder . . . Don't cut me off . . . Hullo? . . . Hullo?'

Maigret stopped most of the onlookers from coming in. But the bargees who had found the corpse and helped to fish it out were all in the café where the tables were still littered with glasses and empty bottles from the day before. The stove was rumbling. There was a broom in the middle of the floor.

Through one of the windows the Chief-Inspector caught sight of the silhouette of Vladimir, who had found time to put on his American sailor cap. The bargees were talking to him, but he was not replying.

The colonel was still gazing at the corpse stretched out on the reddish flagstones and it would have been hard to say whether he was moved or bored or frightened.

'When did you last see him?' asked Maigret, going up to him.

Sir Walter sighed and gave the impression of looking around for the man to whom he usually gave the job of replying for him.

'It's horrible,' he said at last.

'He didn't sleep on board?'

With a wave of the hand the Englishman drew his attention to the bargees who were listening to them. It was like a reminder of the proprieties. It meant:

'Do you think it necessary and proper for these people . . .'

Maigret got them to leave.

'It was ten o'clock last night. . . . There was no whisky left on board . . . Vladimir hadn't found any at Dizy. . . . I decided to go to Épernay . . .'

'Willy went with you?'

'Not for long . . . Just past the bridge he left me. . . .'

'Why?'

'We had a few words . . .'

And while the colonel was saying this, his eyes fixed on the dead man's pale, ravaged, twisted face, his features softened.

Perhaps it was the fact that he had not slept long enough and that his flesh was puffy which made him look moved. In any case Maigret would have sworn that there were tears behind his thick eyelids.

'You quarrelled?'

The colonel shrugged his shoulders, as if resigning himself to this vulgar, commonplace expression.

'You were blaming him for something?'

'No! I wanted to know . . . I kept on saying: "Willy, you're a skunk. . . . But you've got to tell me . . ."'

He fell silent, thoroughly upset, and looked around him to avoid being hypnotized by the dead man.

'You were accusing him of murdering your wife?'

He shrugged his shoulders again and sighed:

'He went off by himself. . . . That happened sometimes. . . . The next day we would drink our first whisky together and forget all about it. . . .'

'You walked all the way to Épernay?'

'Yes.'

'You had a few drinks?'

The colonel gave him a pitying glance.

'I played the tables too, at the club. . . . They had told me at the Bécasse that there was a club. . . . I came back in a taxi. . . .'

'What time was that?'

He indicated with a wave of the hand that he had no idea.

'Willy wasn't in his bunk?'

56

'No . . . Vladimir told me while he was undressing me. . . .'

A motor-cycle with a side-car drew up outside the door. A police-sergeant got off, followed by a doctor. The door opened and shut.

'I'm from Police Headquarters,' said Maigret, introducing himself to his colleague from Épernay. 'Will you keep people away and phone the Public Prosecutor's department. . . .'

The doctor needed only a brief examination to declare:

'He was dead at the time of immersion. . . . Look at these marks. . . .'

Maigret had seen them. He knew. He glanced automatically at the colonel's right hand, which was powerful, with square-cut nails and prominent veins.

*

It would take at least an hour to get the local magistrate and his officials together and bring them to the scene of the crime. Some police cyclists arrived and formed a cordon round the Café de la Marine and the *Southern Cross*.

'May I get dressed?' asked the colonel.

And in spite of his dressing-gown, his slippers, and his bare ankles, he was amazingly dignified as he walked through the crowd of onlookers. He had scarcely gone into the cabin before he put his head out and called:

'Vladimir!'

All the hatchways on the yacht were closed.

Maigret started questioning the lock-keeper, whom a motor-barge was summoning to his gates.

'I suppose there isn't any current in a canal. So that a body is bound to stay where it is thrown in. . . .'

'That's true of the long reaches, of eight or ten miles. . . . But this reach isn't even five miles long. . . . If a boat comes down through Lock 13, above mine, I can feel the water arriving a few minutes later . . . and if I lock through a boat going downstream, I take hundreds of gallons of water from the canal which create a temporary current. . . .'

'What time do you start work?'

'In theory, at sunrise. . . . In fact, much earlier. . . . The stable-barges, which move slowly, leave about three in the morning and generally lock through themselves without us hearing them. . . . We don't say anything, because we know them. . . .'

'So that this morning . . .'

'The *Frédéric*, which spent the night there, must have left about half past three and locked through at Ay at five o'clock. . . .'

Maigret went back the way he had come. A few groups had formed in front of the Café de la Marine and on the tow-path. As the Chief-Inspector passed them, making for the stone bridge, an old pilot with a grog-blossomed nose came up to him.

'Do you want me to show you where the young man was thrown into the water?'

And he gave a proud glance at his friends who hung back.

He was right. Fifty yards from the stone bridge, the reeds were lying flat over a distance of several yards. Not only had somebody walked on them, but a heavy object had been dragged along the ground, for there was a wide trail of flattened reeds.

'See that? . . . I live a quarter of a mile from here, in one of the first houses in Dizy. . . . When I came along this morning, to see if there were any boats going down the Marne that needed me, I was struck by that straight away. . . . Especially as I found this thingummy-bob on the towpath. . . .'

The man was tiresome, with his knowing looks and the glances he kept darting at his companions who were following at a distance.

But the object he took out of his pocket was of the greatest interest. It was a delicately wrought enamel badge which, together with a kedge anchor, bore the initials: Y.C.F.

'Yachting Club de France,' explained the pilot. 'They all wear that in their buttonhole. . . .'

Maigret turned to look at the yacht, which was about a mile away, and, under the words *Southern Cross* made out the same letters: Y.C.F.

Without paying any further attention to his companion, who had handed the badge over to him, he walked slowly as far as the bridge. On the right stretched the Épernay road, absolutely straight, with motor-cars roaring along it. On the left the path bent sharply into the village of Dizy. On the far side of the bridge, on the canal, there were a few barges under repair, in front of the General Navigation Company's yards.

Maigret retraced his steps, feeling a little on edge, because the local magistrate was going to arrive and for an hour or two there would be the usual fuss and bother, questions, comings and goings, ridiculous theories.

When he reached the yacht he found its hatchways still closed. A uniformed policeman was pacing up and down, telling onlookers to keep moving, but unable to prevent a couple of journalists from Épernay from taking photographs.

The weather was neither good nor bad. The sky was a luminous grey, as uniform as a ceiling of frosted glass.

Maigret went up the gangway and knocked on the door.

'Who's there?' asked the colonel's voice.

He went in. He had no desire to waste time talking. He saw the Negretti woman as dishevelled as ever, drying her eyes and snivelling, with her hair hanging down over her cheeks and the back of her neck.

Sir Walter, sitting on the bench, was holding his feet out to Vladimir who was putting a pair of brown shoes on them.

There must have been some water boiling somewhere on a stove, for he could hear a jet of steam.

The colonel's bunk and Gloria's had not been made yet.

And there were playing-cards lying about on the table, as well as a map of the inland waterways of France.

The same vague, spicy smell still hung in the air, recalling at one and the same time bar, boudoir, and bed. A white yachting cap was hanging on the coat-stand, next to an ivory-handled riding-crop.

'Did Willy belong to the Yachting Club de France?' asked Maigret, in a voice which he tried to keep casual.

The colonel's shrug of the shoulders indicated that the question was absurd. As indeed it was, for the Y.C.F. was one of the most exclusive of clubs.

'I do,' said Sir Walter. 'And to the Royal Yacht Club.'

'Would you mind showing me the jacket you were wearing last night?'

'Vladimir . . .'

He had his shoes on. He stood up and bent down to look inside a little cupboard which had been fitted out as a cocktail cabinet. There was no bottle of whisky to be seen in it, but there were some other spirits, between which he hesitated.

Finally he took out a bottle of brandy and murmured casually:

'Will you have some?'

'No, thank you.'

He filled a silver goblet from a rack over the table and looked around for a syphon, frowning like a man whose habits have been disturbed and who cannot get used to it.

Vladimir came back from the bathroom with a black tweed suit and a gesture from his master ordered him to hand it over to Maigret.

'The Y.C.F. badge used to be in the buttonhole of this jacket?'

'Yes . . . Haven't they finished yet? . . . Is Willy still on the floor over there?'

He had emptied his glass, in a series of sips, and was hesitating as to whether to have another.

He glanced out of the port-hole, saw some legs, and gave a muffled groan.

'Will you listen to me for a moment, Colonel?'

He nodded. Maigret took the enamel badge out of his pocket.

'This badge was found this morning at the place where Willy was dragged through the reeds before being pushed into the canal.'

The Negretti woman gave a half-cry, threw herself on to the red velvet bench, and, her head in her hands, started sobbing convulsively.

Vladimir, for his part, did not move. He was waiting for the jacket to be handed back to him so that he could hang it up again in its place.

The colonel gave a peculiar laugh and said four or five times:

'Yes . . . Yes . . .'

At the same time he poured himself another brandy.

'In England the police have a different method of asking questions. . . . They have to remind you that anything you say may be used in evidence against you . . . only once, of course. . . . Haven't you got to write all this down? I shan't go on repeating myself . . .

'We had a few words, Willy and I . . . I kept asking. . . . Never mind . . .

'He isn't a skunk like all the others. . . . There are some likeable skunks . . .

'I said a few harsh things and he grabbed my jacket here. . . .'

He pointed to the lapels, darting an impatient glance at the feet in clogs or heavy shoes which could still be seen through the port-holes.

'That's all . . . I don't know. . . . Perhaps the badge fell on the ground. . . . It was on the far side of the bridge . . .'

'But the badge was found on this side . . .'

Vladimir did not even seem to be listening. He picked

up things that were lying around, disappeared forward, and came sauntering back.

In a strong Russian accent he asked Gloria, who had stopped crying but was lying stretched out, motionless, her head between her hands:

'Do you want anything?'

Footsteps rang out on the gangway. There was a knock on the door and the sergeant's voice said:

'Are you there, Chief-Inspector? . . . It's the Public Prosecutor's department . . .'

'I'm coming!'

The sergeant did not move, invisible behind the mahogany door with the brass handles.

'One more question, Colonel. . . . When is the funeral?'

'At three o'clock.'

'Today?'

'Yes . . . I've got no other reason to stay here.'

When he had drunk his third three-star brandy, his eyes took on that vague expression which Maigret had already seen in them.

And, calm, indifferent, the perfect English gentleman, he asked as the Chief-Inspector was getting up to go:

'Am I under arrest?'

The Negretti woman jerked her head up, deathly pale.

CHAPTER 6

The American Cap

THE end of the conversation between the magistrate and the colonel was almost solemn, and Maigret, who stayed in the background, was not the only one to notice this. The Chief-Inspector's eyes met those of the Public Prosecutor's deputy and read the same feeling in them.

The examining magistrate and his officials had installed themselves in the bar-room of the Café de la Marine. One of the doors opened into the kitchen, where the clatter of saucepans could be heard. The other door, which had a pane of glass covered with transparent advertisements for noodles and rock soap, afforded a glimpse of the bags and crates in the shop.

A policeman's peaked cap passed to and fro outside the window, and farther off a crowd of onlookers was massed, silent but stubborn.

A mug which still contained a little liquid had been left near a pool of wine on one of the tables.

The clerk of the court, a sour expression on his face, was sitting on a bench, writing.

As for the corpse, once the necessary particulars had been taken, it had been deposited in the corner farthest from the stove and temporarily covered with a brown oilcloth taken from a table whose uneven planks were now exposed to view.

The smell was as persistent as ever: spices, stable, tar, wine.

And the magistrate, who had the reputation of being one of the most unpleasant in Épernay – a certain Clair-fontaine de Lagny who prided himself on his noble parti-cules – stood with his back to the fire, polishing his pince-nez.

Right at the start he had said in English:

'I suppose you would rather speak your own language. . . .'

He himself spoke it fluently, with perhaps a touch of affectation, that twisting of the lips common to those who try in vain to acquire the correct accent.

Sir Walter had nodded, had slowly answered all the questions, keeping an eye on the clerk of the court as he wrote and waiting every now and then for the latter to catch up with him.

He had repeated, without adding anything, what he had told Maigret in the course of their two conversations.

For the occasion he had put on a navy-blue suit of almost military cut. In his hand he held a cap with a big gilt crest bearing the arms of the Yatching Club de France.

It was all very simple. One man was asking questions. Another who bowed almost imperceptibly every time before answering.

The fact remained that Maigret was filled with admiration, at the same time feeling a certain humiliation at the memory of his own intrusions on board the *Southern Cross*.

He did not know enough English to grasp the finer shades of meaning. But at least he understood the final exchanges.

'I must ask you, Sir Walter,' said the magistrate, 'to hold yourself at my disposal until these two cases have been cleared up. I also find myself obliged for the moment to refuse permission for the burial of Lady Lampson. . . .'

A nod of the head.

'Have I your permission to leave Dizy with my boat?'

And the colonel waved his hand towards the onlookers gathered outside, the scene around them, the very sky.

'My home is at Porquerolles. . . . It takes me a week just to reach the Saône. . . .'

It was the magistrate's turn to nod his head.

They did not shake hands, but they came close to doing so. The colonel glanced around him, appeared not to see the doctor who looked bored, nor Maigret who turned his head away, and bowed to the Public Prosecutor's deputy.

The next moment he was crossing the narrow space separating the Café de la Marine from the *Southern Cross*.

He did not even go into the cabin. Vladimir was on the deck. He gave him some orders and installed himself at the wheel.

And, to the amazement of the bargees, the seaman in the striped jersey went down into the engine-room, started the engine, and standing on the deck, jerked the mooring-ropes from their bitts with a precise gesture.

A few moments later, a little group of gesticulating figures made off towards the main road, where the motor-cars were waiting: it was the magistrate and his party.

Maigret was left alone on the bank. He had at last been able to fill his pipe, and he thrust his hands into his pockets with a plebeian gesture which was more plebeian than usual, at the same time muttering:–

'As you were!'

For now he had to start all over again.

The magistrate's inquiry had yielded only a few points of detail whose importance it was impossible to judge as yet.

First of all, apart from the marks of strangulation, Willy Marco's body had bruises on the torso and the wrists. According to the doctor, the idea of an ambush had to be rejected in favour of the theory of a fight with an adversary of exceptional strength.

Then Sir Walter had declared that he had met his wife at Nice where, although divorced from an Italian called Ceccaldi, she was still using his name.

The colonel had been vague. His deliberately ambiguous remarks suggested that at that time Marie Dupin, *alias* Ceccaldi, was in a state bordering on poverty and lived on the generosity of a few friends, without actually descending to prostitution.

He had married during a visit to London and it was

c

then that she had had a birth certificate in the name of Marie Dupin sent from France.

'She was an absolutely charming woman . . .'

Maigret recalled the colonel's fleshy, solemn, brick-coloured face while he was saying these words, without any affectation and with a simplicity which the magistrate had seemed to appreciate.

He had to step back to make way for the stretcher which was taking away Willy's body.

And suddenly, shrugging his shoulders, he went into the café, dropped on to a bench, and said:

'A beer!'

*

It was the girl who served him, her eyes still red, her nose shining. He looked at her with interest and, before he could ask her any questions, she looked round to make sure that nobody could hear her and murmured:

'Did he suffer much?'

She had a plain face, thick ankles, plump red arms. She was none the less the only person to worry about the elegant Willy who, the day before, had perhaps given her a playful pinch – if that!

This reminded Maigret of the conversation he had had with the young man, half stretched out on the unmade bed upstairs, and smoking one cigarette after another.

The girl was called somewhere else. A bargee said to her:

'Seems you're proper upset, Emma. . . .'

And she tried to smile, giving Maigret a conspiratorial glance.

Traffic on the canal had stopped since the morning. There were seven boats, including three motor-barges, opposite the Café de la Marine. The women came across to do their shopping and every time the shop-bell tinkled.

'You can have your lunch whenever you like,' the proprietor told Maigret.

'In a few minutes.'

And from the doorway he looked at the place where only that morning the *Southern Cross* had been moored.

In the evening two fit, healthy men had come off the yacht. They had set off in the direction of the stone bridge. If the colonel was to be believed, they had parted after a quarrel and Sir Walter had continued on his way along the straight, deserted road, two or three miles long, which led to the first houses in Épernay.

Nobody had seen Willy alive again. When the colonel had come back, in a taxi, he had not noticed anything unusual.

No witnesses. Nobody had heard anything. The Dizy butcher, who lived about a quarter of a mile from the bridge said that his dog had barked, but as he had not worried about this, he could not say what time it had been.

The tow-path, with its puddles and pools, had been trodden by too many men and horses for any useful tracks to be found on it.

The previous Thursday, Mary Lampson, likewise fit and healthy, and in an apparently normal state of mind, had left the *Southern Cross*, where she was alone.

Beforehand – according to Willy – she had handed her lover a pearl necklace, the only valuable she possessed.

And all traces of her had been lost. Nowhere had she been seen again alive. Two days had gone by without so much as a glimpse of her.

On the Sunday evening she was strangled, hidden under the straw in a stable at Dizy, sixty miles from her point of departure, and two carters spent the night snoring beside her corpse.

And that was all. On the magistrate's orders, the two bodies were going to be placed in a refrigerator at the mortuary.

The *Southern Cross* had just left on its way to the south, to Porquerolles, to the Petit Langoustier which had seen so many orgies.

Head down, Maigret walked around the buildings of

the Café de la Marine. He pushed away a furious goose which came at him with its beak open in a hoarse cry of anger.

There was no lock on the stable door, just an ordinary wooden latch. And the gun-dog prowling round the yard, its paunch over-filled, rushed to meet every visitor, circling round them in joy.

Opening the door, the Chief-Inspector found himself face to face with the proprietor's grey horse, which was as unattached as it had been on other days and which took the opportunity to go for a canter outside.

The broken-kneed mare was still lying sad-eyed in her stall.

Maigret pushed the straw with his foot, as if he hoped to find something which had escaped his notice on his first examination of the place.

Two or three times he muttered crossly to himself:

'As you were!'

He had almost made up his mind to go back to Meaux, even to Paris, and retrace step by step the route taken by the *Southern Cross*.

All sorts of odds and ends were lying around: old reins, pieces of harness, a candle-end, a broken pipe . . .

From a distance he saw something white sticking out of a pile of hay and he went over to it without much hope. The next moment he was holding an American sailor's cap like Vladimir's.

The material was covered with mud and dung, and twisted as if it had been pulled in all directions.

But it was in vain that Maigret hunted around for another clue. Some clean straw had been thrown over the place where the body had been found, to make it less sinister.

'*Am I under arrest?*'

He could not have explained why that question of the colonel's should have come back to him while he was making for the stable door. At the same time he pictured Sir Walter to himself, at once aristocratic and besotted, with his big moist eyes, his latent drunkenness, his astonishing calm.

He remembered his brief dialogue with the snobbish magistrate in that bar-room full of tables covered with brown oilcloth which the magic of a few intonations, a few attitudes, had transformed for a moment into a drawing-room.

And he twisted the cap about in his hands suspiciously, a sly look in his eyes.

'Go cautiously!' Monsieur de Clairfontaine de Lagny had told him, giving him a perfunctory handshake.

The goose, in a ferocious mood, was following the horse around and screaming abuse at it, while it hung its big head and sniffed at the rubbish littering the yard.

On either side of the door there was a corner-stone, and the Chief-Inspector sat down on one of them, without letting go of the cap, or of his cold pipe.

In front of him there was nothing but a huge pile of manure, then a hedge with gaps in it here and there, and beyond that, fields where nothing was growing yet and the hill streaked with black and white on which a cloud with a jet-black centre seemed to be pressing with all its weight.

From one edge came an oblique ray of sunshine which put sparks of light on the manure.

'*A charming woman,*' the colonel had said of Mary Lampson.

'*A real gentleman,*' Willy had said of the colonel.

Only Vladimir had said nothing, simply coming and going, buying food and petrol, filling the water tanks with drinking-water, baling out the dinghy, and helping his master to dress.

Some Flemings went by along the road, talking loudly. Suddenly Maigret bent forward. The yard was paved with uneven stones. And six feet away, between two of them, something had just been caught by the sun and was gleaming brightly.

It was a gold cuff-link crossed by two threads of platinum. Maigret had seen a pair of similar cuff-links at Willy's wrists the day before, when the young man had been lying on his bed, blowing the smoke from his cigarettes at the ceiling and talking nonchalantly.

From then on he paid no further attention to the horse or the goose or anything else around him. A little later he was turning the handle of the telephone.

'Épernay. . . . Yes, the mortuary. . . . This is a police call . . .'

One of the Flemings, who was coming out of the café, stopped to look at him in astonishment, he was so excited.

'Hullo! . . . Chief-Inspector Maigret here, from Police Headquarters. . . . A body has just been brought along to you . . . No, I'm not talking about the motor accident. . . . The drowned man from Dizy. . . . Yes. . . . Go to the office straight away and have a look at his personal effects. . . . You ought to find a cuff-link there. . . . Tell me what it's like . . . I'll wait, yes. . . .'

Three minutes later he hung up, satisfied, still holding the cap and the cuff-link in one hand.

'Your lunch is ready. . . .'

He did not bother to answer the red-headed girl, for all that she had said that to him as sweetly as possible. He went out, feeling that he might be holding the key to the mystery, but at the same time terrified of dropping it.

'The cap in the stable. . . . The cuff-link in the yard. . . . And the Y.C.F. badge near the stone bridge. . . .'

It was in that direction that he started walking, striding out. Theories took shape in his mind, only to collapse.

Before he had covered a mile he looked in front of him in amazement.

The *Southern Cross*, which had left a good hour before in tremendous haste, was moored to the right of the bridge, in the reeds. There was no sign of anybody.

But when the Chief-Inspector was only a hundred yards away, on the opposite bank, a motor-car coming from Épernay drew up near the yacht and Vladimir, still in his seaman's jersey, who was sitting beside the driver, jumped out and ran towards the boat.

Before he reached it the hatchway opened and the colonel came out on deck, holding his hand out to somebody inside.

Maigret made no attempt to conceal himself. He could not tell whether the colonel had seen him or not.

The scene was brief. The Chief-Inspector could not hear what was being said. But the characters' movements gave him a fairly clear idea of what was happening.

It was the Negretti woman that Sir Walter was helping out of the cabin. For the first time Maigret saw her wearing outdoor clothes. Even from a distance he could see that she was in a rage.

Vladimir had picked up a couple of suitcases which were waiting and was carrying them to the taxi.

The captain held his hand out to the woman to help her down the gangway, but she refused to take it and rushed forward so abruptly that she nearly fell head-first into the reeds.

And she walked on without waiting for him. He followed her impassively a few paces behind. She threw herself into the taxi with the same fury, put her head out of the window for a moment, and shouted something which must have been an insult or a threat.

Yet Sir Walter bowed courteously as the taxi moved off, then watched it disappear, and came back towards his boat with Vladimir.

Maigret had not stirred. He had a very definite impression that a change was taking place in the Englishman. He did not smile. He was still as calm as ever. But, to take one example, just as he got to the wheel-house, still talking, he touched Vladimir's shoulder with a friendly, even affectionate gesture.

And the manoeuvre was superb. There were only the two men left on board. The Russian pulled in the gangway and with a single movement jerked the ring-bolts of the mooring-ropes free.

71

The bow of the *Southern Cross* was embedded in the reeds. A barge was coming up astern and sounded its hooter.

Lampson turned round. He must almost certainly have seen Maigret, but he gave no sign of it. With one hand he put the engine into gear. With the other he gave the brass wheel a couple of turns and the yacht glided astern, just far enough to free itself, avoided the stem of the barge, stopped in time and moved off again, leaving behind a trail of bubbling foam.

She had not gone a hundred yards before she gave three hoots to warn the lock at Ay of her arrival.

*

'Keep going . . . Straight ahead. . . . Catch up with that taxi if you can . . .'

Maigret had stopped a baker's van which was going towards Épernay. The Negretti woman's taxi could be seen about a mile away, but it was moving fairly slowly, for the surface of the road was greasy and slippery.

As soon as the Chief-Inspector had revealed his identity, the delivery-man had looked at him with amused curiosity.

'You know, it wouldn't take me five minutes to catch up with them. . . .'

'Not too fast. . . .'

And it was Maigret's turn to smile at seeing his companion hunching himself over the wheel like a detective in pursuit of a criminal in an American film.

There were no dangerous manoeuvres to carry out, no difficulties to overcome. In one of the first streets in the town the taxi stopped for a few moments, presumably to allow the woman to confer with the driver, then moved off again, drawing up three minutes later in front of a fairly luxurious hotel.

Maigret got out of his van a hundred yards away and thanked the baker, who refused to accept a tip but, determined to see a bit more, went and parked close to the hotel.

A porter carried in the two suitcases. Gloria Negretti hurried across the pavement.

Ten minutes later the Chief-Inspector asked to see the manager.

'The lady who has just arrived?'

'Room 9. . . . I guessed there was something fishy . . . I've never seen anybody so worked up. . . . She jabbered away incredibly fast, using a lot of foreign words . . . I gathered that she didn't want to be disturbed and that she wanted a packet of cigarettes and some Kümmel taken up to her room. . . . There won't be any scandal, I hope?'

'None whatever,' Maigret assured him. 'I just want to ask her a few questions. . . .'

He could not help smiling as he approached the door marked with a figure 9. For there was an absolute din coming from the room. The young woman's high heels were clattering up and down the floor.

She was walking around in all directions. He could hear her shutting a window, moving a suitcase around, turning on a tap, throwing herself on the bed, getting up, and finally hurling a shoe to the other end of the room.

Maigret knocked on the door.

'Come in!'

The voice was shaking with anger and impatience. The Negretti woman had not been there ten minutes and yet she had had time to change her clothes, rumple her hair, and altogether resume, in a more rejected form, the appearance she had on board the *Southern Cross*.

When she recognized the Chief-Inspector, there was a glint of anger in her brown eyes.

'What do you want? . . . What have you come here for? . . . This is my room . . . I've paid for it and . . .'

She went on in a foreign language, presumably Spanish, and opened a bottle of eau-de-Cologne, pouring the greater part of the contents over her hands before moistening her burning forehead with it.

'May I ask you a question?'

'I told them I didn't want to see anybody. . . . Get out! . . . Do you hear?'

She was walking in her stockinged feet, and presumably her silk stockings had no garters, for they started to slip down her legs, already revealing a very pale, fleshy knee.

'You'd do better to keep your questions for those who can answer them. . . . But you don't dare to, do you? . . . Because he's a colonel. . . Because he's *Sir* Walter. . . . A fine *sir* he is . . . Why, if I told you only half of what I know. . . . Look at this. . . .'

She rummaged feverishly in her handbag and took out five crumpled thousand-franc notes.

'That's what he's just given me! . . . And I've lived with him for two years, I've . . .'

She threw the notes on to the carpet, then, changing her mind, picked them up and put them back in her handbag.

'Of course he promised to send me a cheque. . . . But I know what his promises are worth. . . . A cheque? . . . He won't even have enough money to get as far as Porquerolles. . . . Not that that will stop him getting drunk on whisky every day . . .'

She was not crying and yet there were tears in her voice. There was something very special about the hysteria of this woman whom Maigret had always seen steeped in blissful lethargy, in a hot-house atmosphere.

'His precious Vladimir's the same. . . . He had the nerve to say "Good-bye, Madame" while he was trying to kiss my hand. . . . They've got a gift for that sort of thing. . . . But when the colonel wasn't there, Vladimir used to . . .

'That's none of your business. . . . Why do you go on standing there? . . . What are you waiting for? Are you hoping I'm going to tell you something? Not a thing! All the same, you've got to admit I'd be in my rights if I did. . . .'

She kept on moving around, taking things out of her suitcase and putting them down somewhere, only to pick them up again and place them somewhere else.

'Leaving me at Épernay. . . . In this filthy rainy hole. . . . I begged him to take me at least to Nice, where I have friends. . . . It was for his sake that I left them . . .

'It's true that I ought to be glad that he hasn't killed me. . . .

'I'm not saying anything, mind you. . . . You can clear out . . . I loathe the police! . . . As much as the English. . . . If you're capable of doing it, go and arrest him. . . .

'But you wouldn't dare! . . . I know only too well how these things are arranged. . . .

'Poor Mary! . . . People can say what they like about her. Of course she had a bad temper, of course she'd have done anything for that Willy I've never been able to stand. . . .

'But to die like that . . .

'Have they gone? . . . Then who are you going to arrest in the end? . . . Me, perhaps? Why not? . . .

'Well, listen. . . . I'm going to tell you something after all. . . . Just one little thing. . . . You can do what you like with it. . . . This morning, when he was dressing up for the magistrate – because he's always got to impress people – Walter told Vladimir, in Russian, because he thinks I don't understand that language . . .'

She was talking so fast that she was beginning to run out of breath, getting tongue-tied and using Spanish words again.

'He told him to try to find out where the *Providence* was. . . . You understand. . . . It's a barge that was near us at Meaux. . . .

'They want to catch up with it and they're afraid of me. . . .

'I pretended I hadn't heard . . .

'But I know perfectly well you wouldn't dare . . .'

She looked at her open suitcases, at the room which in a few minutes she had managed to turn upside down and fill with her pungent scent. . . .

'Have you got a cigarette at least? . . . What sort of

75

hotel is this? . . . I ordered a packet of cigarettes and some Kümmel . . .'

'Did you see the colonel talking to anybody from the *Providence* at Meaux?'

'I didn't see anything. . . . I wasn't taking any notice. . . . I just heard what he said this morning. . . . Why should they bother about a barge, otherwise? . . . Does anybody know how Walter's first wife died, out in India? . . . And if the other one got a divorce, she probably had her reasons. . . .'

A waiter knocked on the door, bringing cigarettes and liqueur. The Negretti woman took the packet and flung it out into the corridor, shouting:

'I said *Abdullahs*!'

'But Madame . . .'

She clasped her hands together in a gesture which suggested that an attack of hysterics was not far off. and groaned:

'Oh! . . . These people! . . . These . . .'

She turned towards Maigret who was looking at her with interest and snarled at him:

'Why are you still waiting here? . . . I'm not saying any more! I don't know anything! I haven't said anything! . . . You understand? . . . I don't want to be bothered with this business. . . . It's bad enough that I've wasted two years of my life. . . .'

The waiter, as he left the room, gave a meaning look at the Chief-Inspector. And when the young woman, her nerves frayed out, threw herself on to her bed, Maigret went out too.

In the street the baker was still waiting.

'What? You haven't arrested her?' he asked, looking disappointed. 'I thought . . .'

Maigret had to walk as far as the station to find a taxi to drive him back to the stone bridge.

CHAPTER 7

The Pedal

WHEN the Chief-Inspector passed the *Southern Cross,* whose
wash went on stirring the reeds long after she had gone
by, the colonel was still at the wheel and Vladimir was
standing forward, coiling a rope.

Maigret waited for the yacht at Aigny Lock. The
manœuvre was carried out without a hitch, and once the
boat had been moored the Russian went ashore to produce
her papers and give the lock-keeper a tip.

'This cap *is* yours, isn't it?' the Chief-Inspector asked,
going up to him.

Vladimir examined the cap, which was now just a dirty
rag, then his questioner.

'Thank you,' he said at last, taking the cap.

'Just a moment! Can you tell me when you lost it?'

The colonel was following the scene without betraying
the slightest emotion.

'It fell into the water last night,' explained Vladimir,
'when I was leaning over the stern, using a boat-hook to
clear away some weeds that were fouling the propeller. . . .
There was a barge behind us. . . . The woman was kneeling in the dinghy, rinsing her washing. . . . She fished
the cap out of the water and I left it on the deck to dry
out. . . .'

'In other words, it was on the deck last night?'

'Yes. . . . This morning I didn't notice it had gone.'

'Was it already dirty yesterday?'

'No. When the woman fished it out, she dipped it in
the soap-suds she was using. . . .'

The yacht was rising jerkily and already the lock-keeper
was holding the wheel of the upstream gate with both
hands.

'If I remember rightly, it was the *Phénix* behind you, wasn't it?'

'I think so. . . . I haven't seen her again today. . . .'

Maigret gave a wave of the hand and went back to his bicycle while the colonel, as impassive as ever, started up the engine and nodded his head as he passed the lock-keeper.

The Chief-Inspector stood for a while, thoughtfully watching him move away, and disturbed by the amazing simplicity with which things happened on board the *Southern Cross*.

The yacht continued on its way without troubling about him. At the very most the colonel, from his position at the wheel, put a question to the Russian, who answered with a single phrase.

'Is the *Phénix* far ahead?' asked Maigret.

'She may be in the Juvigny reach, three miles from here. . . . She doesn't move as fast as that thing. . . .'

Maigret arrived there a few moments before the *Southern Cross*, and Vladimir must have seen him, from a distance, questioning the skipper's wife.

The details were correct. The day before, while she was rinsing her washing, which could be seen, puffed out by the wind, on a wire stretched above the barge, she had fished the seaman's cap out of the water. A little later the man had given her boy two francs.

It was four o'clock in the afternoon. The Chief-Inspector got back on his bicycle, his head heavy with vague theories. There was some gravel on the tow-path and the tyres crunched over it, sending little pebbles flying on both sides of the wheels.

At Lock 9 Maigret had a good start on the Englishman.

'Can you tell me where the *Providence* is now?'

'Not far from Vitry-le-François. They're going at a good speed, because they've some fine horses, and above all a carter who isn't afraid of work. . . .'

'Do they seem to be hurrying?'

'No more and no less than usual. On the canal, you know, folk are always in a hurry. . . . You never know what's ahead of you. . . . You can lose hours at a single lock just as you can spend ten minutes . . . and the faster you go, the more you earn. . . .'

'You didn't hear anything unusual last night?'

'No. . . . Why? . . . Was there something?'

Maigret went off without answering, and after that stopped at every lock, at every boat.

He had had no difficulty in summing up Gloria Negretti. While refusing to say anything whatever against the colonel she had in fact come out with everything she knew.

For she was incapable of keeping anything back. Incapable of lying too. Or if not, she would have invented something infinitely more complicated.

So she really had heard Sir Walter ask Vladimir to find out where the *Providence* was.

Now the Chief-Inspector too was interested in this barge which had arrived on the Sunday evening, not long before Mary Lampson's death, coming from Meaux, and which, being a wooden boat, was coated with resin.

Why did the colonel want to catch up with her? What connexion was there between the *Southern Cross* and the heavy boat moving at the slow pace of her two horses?

Bowling along through the monotonous canal scenery and bearing down more and more wearily on the pedals, Maigret went on sketching out theories, but they led him only to fragmentary or unacceptable conclusions.

Yet didn't the Negretti woman's angry accusation throw some light on the matter of the three clues?

A score of times Maigret had tried to reconstruct the movements of the various characters in the drama, in the course of that night about which nothing was known, except that Willy Marco was dead.

Every time he had been conscious of a gap; he had had the impression that there was a character missing, who was neither the colonel, nor the dead man, nor Vladimir . . .

And now the *Southern Cross* was going after somebody on board the *Providence*.

Somebody who had obviously been involved in the recent events. Wasn't it reasonable to assume that that somebody had taken part in the second drama, namely the murder of Willy, as well as the first?

It is possible to cover a considerable distance in a short time at night, on a bicycle for example, keeping to a tow-path.

'Did you hear anything last night? . . . Did you notice anything unusual on board the *Providence* when she went past?'

It was thankless, disappointing work, especially in the thin drizzle which was falling from the low-lying clouds.

'No, nothing . . .'

The gap was widening between Maigret and the *Southern Cross*, which was losing at least twenty minutes at every lock. The Chief-Inspector got back on his bicycle more wearily every time, and stubbornly picked up one of the threads of his reasoning in the solitude of a reach.

He had already covered twenty-five miles when the lock-keeper at Sarry answered his question.

'My dog barked . . . I think something must have gone past along the road. . . . A rabbit perhaps. . . . I went back to sleep straight away. . . .'

'Do you know where the *Providence* spent the night?'

The man did a sum in his head.

'Wait a minute. Wouldn't be surprised if she'd got as far as Pogny. . . . The skipper wanted to be at Vitry-le-François tonight. . . .'

Another two locks. And no luck. Maigret had to follow the lock-keepers on to their gates, for the farther he went, the heavier he found the traffic. At Vésigneul three boats were waiting their turn. At Pogny there were five.

'Noise? No,' growled the keeper at this last lock. 'But I'd like to know who had the nerve to use my bike. . . .'

The Chief-Inspector mopped his brow at this hint of

a clue. He was breathless and parched. He had just covered thirty miles without drinking so much as a glass of beer.

'Where is your bicycle?'

'Open the sluices yourself, will you, François,' the lock-keeper called out to a carter.

And he led Maigret towards his house. In the kitchen, which opened on to the tow-path, some bargees were drinking white wine which a woman was pouring out for them without letting go of her baby.

'You aren't going to report me, I hope? We aren't allowed to sell wine. . . . But everybody does it. . . . It's really just to do people a service. . . . Here we are . . .'

He pointed to a wooden shed built against a wall. There was no door.

'This is the bike. . . . It's my wife's. . . . Just imagine, the nearest grocer's shop is two miles from here. . . . I keep telling her to bring the bike inside for the night, but she says it dirties the house. . . . Mind you, the chap who used it is a queer sort of cuss. . . . I might never have noticed anything. . . .

'As it happens, the day before yesterday my nephew, who's a mechanic at Rheims, came here for the day. . . . The chain was broken. . . . He mended it and while he was at it he cleaned the bike thoroughly and oiled it. . . .

'Yesterday nobody used it. . . . Oh, and the back wheel had been fitted with a new tyre too. . . .

'Well, this morning the bike was perfectly clean, although it rained all night. . . . You've seen the mud on the tow-path. . . .

'But the left pedal is out of truth and the tyre looks as if it had done at least fifty miles. . . .

'Can you make anything of it? . . . The bike has travelled, that's certain. . . . And the chap who brought it back took the trouble to clean it. . . .'

'What are the boats which spent the night near here?'

'Wait a minute. . . . The *Madeleine* must have gone to La

Chaussée, where the skipper's brother-in-law keeps a pub
– The *Miséricorde* spent the night below my lock. . . .'

'Has she come from Dizy?'

'No. She's come downstream from the Saône. . . . There's
only the *Providence*. . . . She locked through yesterday at
seven in the evening. . . . She went on to Omey, a mile
from here, where there's a good port. . . .'

'Have you got another bicycle?'

'No. . . . But I can still use this one. . . .'

'I'm afraid not. I want you to lock it up somewhere . . .'
Hire another if necessary. . . . I'm counting on you.'

The bargees were coming out of the kitchen and one of
them called out to the lock-keeper:

'Is that how you entertain your friends, Désiné?'

'Just a minute. . . . I'm talking to this gentleman. . .

'Where do you think I can catch up with the *Providence*?'

'Well, she's still going at a good speed. . . . I'd be surprised if you caught up with her before Vitry. . . .'

Maigret was going to set off. He came back, took a
spanner out of his tool-bag, and removed the two pedals
from the lock-keeper's bicycle.

When he left, the pedals, which he had stuffed into his
pockets, made two lumps in his jacket.

*

The lock-keeper at Dizy had told him jokingly:

'When it's fine everywhere else, there are at least two
places where you can be sure to see it raining: here and
Vitry-le-François. . . .'

Maigret was approaching this town and it started raining
again: a thin, lazy, steady drizzle.

The appearance of the canal was changing. There were
factories along the banks and for a long time the Chief-
Inspector threaded his way through a swarm of working-
girls coming out of one of them.

Almost everywhere there were boats unloading and
others waiting half-empty.

And there were some little suburban houses again with rabbit hutches made out of old crates, and pathetic gardens.

Every mile there was a cement factory or a quarry or a lime-kiln. And the rain was mixing the white powder in the air with the mud on the tow-path. The cement shrouded everything: the tiled roofs, the apple-trees, and the grass.

Maigret was beginning to adopt that movement from right to left and left to right which is the mark of the tired cyclist. He was thinking without thinking. He kept lining up ideas which it was not yet possible to bring together in a solid bundle.

When he finally caught sight of the lock at Vitry-le-François, darkness was falling, speckled with the white lights of about sixty boats in Indian file.

Some were overtaking others, or broaching to. And when a barge approached in the opposite direction, shouts, oaths, and messages filled the air.

'Hey, there! . . . *The Simoun!* . . . We saw your sister-in-law at Chalon-sur-Saône, and she asked us to tell you that she'll see you on the Burgundy canal. . . . The christening can wait. . . . Pierre sends his regards. . . .'

On the lock gates there were about a dozen figures bustling around.

And over everything, a bluish, rainy mist, in which the silhouettes of motionless horses could be made out, and men going from one boat to another.

While Maigret was reading the names on the sterns of the barges, a voice called out to him:

'Good evening, Monsieur!'

It took him a few seconds to recognize the skipper of the *Éco III*.

'Repairs finished already?'

'It was nothing! . . . My boy's a fool. . . . The mechanic who came from Rheims took only five minutes over it.'

'You haven't seen the *Providence*, have you?'

'She's ahead of us. . . . But we'll go through before her

for all that. . . . This jam means that we'll be locking
through all night and maybe tomorrow night too. . . . Just
imagine, there are at least sixty boats here and they're still
coming. . . . Generally speaking, motor-barges have precedence over horse-barges. . . . This time, the engineer has
decided to lock us through alternately, one horse-barge and
then one motor-barge. . . .'

And the man, a likeable fellow with an open face, pointed
into the distance.

'Look! . . . Just opposite the crane. . . . I can recognize
her white tiller. . . .'

Passing the barges, Maigret could see, through the
hatchways, people eating in the yellow light of oil-lamps.

Maigret found the skipper of the *Providence* on the quay-
side, deep in discussion with some other bargees.

'Of course the motor-barges shouldn't have precedence
over us! . . . Take the *Marie*, for instance. . . . We gain a
mile over her in a five-mile reach, but with this system
she'll lock through ahead of us. . . . Why, it's the Chief-
Inspector!'

And the little man held out his hand, as he would to
a friend.

'Are you here with us again? . . . The missus is on
board. . . . She'll be pleased to see you again, because she
says that, as coppers go, you're a good sort. . . .'

In the darkness the red tips of cigarettes could be seen
glowing, and the lamps so close to one another that it was
a mystery how the boats could still move about.

Maigret found the plump woman from Brussels straining
her soup. She wiped her hand on her apron before holding
it out to him.

'You haven't found the murderer yet?'

'I'm afraid not. . . . I've come to ask you for some more
information. . . .'

'Sit down. . . . Will you have a drop of something?'

'No, thank you.'

'You can't mean that! . . . Come, now! In this sort of

weather, it can't hurt anybody.... At least you haven't come from Dizy, on a bike, have you?'

'Yes, I have.'

'But that's over forty miles!'

'Is your carter here?'

'He must be at the lock, arguing... They want to cheat us of our turn, and this isn't the moment to give in, because we've already lost enough time....'

'Has he got a bicycle?'

'Who? Jean?... No!'

She laughed, and then explained, going back to her work:

'I can't see him riding a bike, with his little legs.... My husband's got one.... But he hasn't used it for at least a year, and I think the tyres are punctured....'

'You spent last night at Omey?'

'That's right. We always try to moor at a place where I can do my shopping.... Because if you're unlucky enough to stop during the day, there are always some other boats that will pass you....'

'What time did you arrive?'

'About this time. We pay more attention to the sun than the time, you know... Another little drop?... It's some gin we bring back from Belgium on every trip....'

'Did you go to the grocers?'

'Yes, while the men were having their apéritifs.... It must have been just after eight that we turned in....'

'Jean was in the stable?'

'Where else would he have been?... He's only happy when he's with his horses....'

'You didn't hear any noise during the night?'

'Not a thing.... At three o'clock, as usual, Jean came along to make the coffee.... He always does that.... Then we moved off....'

'You didn't notice anything out of the ordinary?'

'What do you mean?... You don't suspect old Jean, I hope?... You know, he looks a bit odd when you don't

know him. . . . But he's been with us now for eight
years. . . . And, well, if he left us, the *Providence* would
never be the same again. . . .'

'Does your husband sleep with you?'

She laughed again. And as Maigret was close to her, she
gave him a dig in the ribs.

'Get along with you! Do we look as old as all that?'

'Can I have a look at the stable?'

'If you like. . . . Take the lantern that's on the deck. . . .
The horses have been left outside because we still hope to
lock through tonight. . . . And once we've got to Vitry,
we're all right. . . . Most of the boats take the Marne canal
to the Rhine. . . . It's quieter towards Saône. . . . Except for
that five-mile tunnel that always frightens me. . . .'

Maigret went by himself towards the middle of the barge
where the stable was to be found. Picking up the storm-
lantern which served as a navigation-light, he stole into
Jean's domain, with its warm smell of dung and leather.

But it was in vain that he floundered about in it for a
quarter of an hour, hearing all the time the conversation
continuing on the quay-side between the skipper of the
Providence and the bargees.

When he arrived a little later at the lock, where, to make
up for lost time, everybody was working at once in a din
of rusty machinery and bubbling water, he caught sight of
the carter on one of the gates, his whip round his neck like
a collar, working a sluice.

As at Dizy, he was dressed in an old corduroy velvet suit
and a faded felt hat which had long ago lost its ribbon.

A barge left the lock, propelled along by a boat-hook,
for there was no other way of moving among the crowded
boats.

The voices calling from one barge to another were hoarse
and bad-tempered, and the faces, which were sometimes lit
up by a match, deeply marked by fatigue.

All these people had been on the move since three or
four in the morning, and dreamed of nothing but their

soup and then the bunks on to which they would finally drop.

But every one of them wanted to make the crowded lock first, so as to be able to start the following day's journey under the most favourable conditions.

The lock-keeper bustled to and fro, grabbing people's papers as he passed, running into his office where he signed and stamped them, and thrusting the tips he was given into his pocket.

'Excuse me . . .'

Maigret had touched the carter's arm. The man turned round slowly and looked at him with his eyes almost hidden behind his thick bushy brows.

'Have you got any other boots than those you are wearing?'

Jean did not seem to understand at first. His face wrinkled up more than ever. He stared at his feet in bewilderment.

Finally he shook his head, took his pipe out of his mouth, and simply murmured:

'Any others?'

'Those are the only boots you've got?'

A slow nod of the head.

'Can you ride a bike?'

Some people drew near, intrigued by this conversation.

'Come along here,' said Maigret. 'I want a word with you. . . .'

The carter followed him in the direction of the *Providence*, which was moored about two hundred yards away. As he passed his horses, which were standing in the rain with their heads down and their backs gleaming, he stroked the neck of the one nearer to him.

'Come on board. . . .'

The skipper, a thin, tiny figure, was pushing at a boat-hook stuck in the canal bed and levering his boat against the bank to allow a barge going downstream to pass.

He saw the two men going into the stable, but he had no time to pay any attention.

'Did you sleep here last night?'

A grunt which meant yes.

'All night? You didn't borrow a bike from the lock-keeper at Pogny?'

The carter had the unhappy look of a simpleton who is being teased or of a dog which has always been kindly treated and which is suddenly beaten for no reason.

He pushed his hat back and rubbed his head, which was covered with white hair as hard as bristles.

'Take your boots off.'

The man did not move, but glanced at the bank where the horses' legs could be seen. One of them neighed as if it had realized that the carter was in difficulties.

'Your boots. . . . Quick!'

And suiting the action to the word, Maigret made Jean sit down on a plank running along one of the walls of the stable.

Only then did the old man become submissive, and, looking reproachfully at his tormentor, he set about taking off one of his boots.

He was not wearing socks, but strips of cloth greased with tallow were wound round his feet and ankles, so that they seemed inseparable from his skin.

The lantern shed only a dim light. The skipper, who had finished his manoeuvre, came and squatted on the deck to see what was happening in the stable.

While Jean, scowling angrily, was lifting up his other leg, Maigret used some straw to clean the sole of the boot he was holding.

Then he took the left pedal out of his pocket and fitted it against the boot.

The bewildered old man gazing at his feet was a strange sight. His trousers, which must have been made for a man even shorter than himself, or which had been cut down, reached only half-way down his legs.

And the strips of greasy cloth were a dark grey, pitted with dirt and bits of straw.

Standing close to the lamp, Maigret compared the pedal, some of the treads of which were broken, with the scarcely visible marks on the leather.

'You took the lock-keeper's bicycle at Pogny last night!' he said slowly and accusingly, without taking his eyes off the two objects. 'How far did you go?'

'Hey, there! The *Providence*! Move up! The *Étourneau* has given up her turn and she's spending the night in the reach. . . .'

Jean turned towards the people moving about outside, then towards the Chief-Inspector.

'You can go and make your lock,' said Maigret. 'Here! Put your boots on. . . .'

The skipper was already wielding his boat-hook. His wife came running up.

'Jean! . . . The horses! . . . If we miss our turn. . . .'

The carter slipped his legs into his boots, hoisted himself up on deck, and called out in a curious voice:

'Ho! Gee up!'

And the horses snorted and moved off, while he jumped ashore and slowly followed behind them, his whip still round his neck.

'Ho! Gee up!'

While her husband pushed with the boat-hook, the woman bore with her whole weight on the wheel so as to avoid the barge coming in the opposite direction, whose rounded stem and haloed lantern at the stern were scarcely visible.

The lock-keeper's impatient voice shouted:

'What's the matter, the *Providence*? Are you going to take all night?'

She glided silently forward over the dark water. But she bumped into the stone wall three times before slipping into the lock, occupying its entire breadth.

CHAPTER 8

Ward 10

USUALLY the four sluices of a lock are opened only one after another, little by little, to avoid the wash which might break the boat's mooring-ropes.

But sixty barges were waiting. The bargees whose turn was approaching were helping to work the machinery, leaving the lock-keeper nothing to do but stamp their papers.

Maigret was on the quayside, holding his bicycle with one hand, and watching the shadows moving about in the darkness. The two horses had stopped of their own accord fifty yards from the upstream gates. Jean was turning one of the wheels.

The water poured in with a torrential din. It could be seen, all white, in the narrow gaps left by the *Providence*.

Suddenly, just as the flood was reaching its height, there was a muffled cry, followed by a thud on the bow of the barge and a confused hubbub.

The Chief-Inspector guessed rather than saw what happened. The carter was no longer in his place on the gate. And the others were running along the walls. Everybody was shouting at once.

There were only two lamps to light up the scene: one in the middle of the lift-bridge before the lock, the other on the barge which was continuing to rise fast.

'Shut the sluices!'

'Open the gates!'

Somebody passed with a huge boat-hook which hit Maigret in the face.

Some bargees came running up. And the lock-keeper came out of his office, panic-stricken at the idea of his responsibility for the accident.

'What is it?'

'The old man . . .'

On either side of the barge, between the boat and the wall, there was not more than a foot of water. And this water, coming from the sluices, was surging and foaming into the narrow space.

There were some clumsy blunders. For instance somebody opened one of the sluices in the downstream gate, and this gate could be heard straining at its hinges while the lock-keeper rushed to repair the damage.

It was only later that the Chief-Inspector learnt that the whole reach could have been flooded and fifty barges damaged.

'Can you see him?'

'There's something dark down there.'

The barge was still rising, but more slowly. Three sluices out of four had been closed. But every few moments the boat thudded against the side of the lock, possibly crushing the carter.

'What depth?'

'At least three foot under the boat.'

It was horrifying. In the feeble glow of the stable-lantern, the skipper's wife could be seen running in all directions with a lifebelt in her hand.

She wailed plaintively:

'I don't think he can swim!'

And Maigret heard a solemn voice near him say:

'All the better! He won't have suffered so much. . . .'

*

All this lasted a quarter of an hour. Three times people thought they saw a body coming to the surface. But it was in vain that boat-hooks were plunged into the water at the places indicated.

The *Providence* slowly emerged from the lock and an old carter muttered:

'I'll bet you anything you like he's caught under the tiller. I've seen that happen at Verdun. . . .'

He was wrong. The barge had scarcely come to a stop fifty yards farther on before some men who were poking at the downstream gate with a pole called for help.

A dinghy had to be brought up. They could feel something under the water, about three feet deep. And just as somebody was getting ready to dive in, while his wife, with tears in her eyes, tried to hold him back, a body suddenly rose to the surface.

It was hauled out of the water. A dozen hands at once grasped the corduroy jacket, which was torn, for it had caught on one of the bolts on the gate.

The rest was like a nightmare. The telephone could be heard ringing in the lock-keeper's house. A boy had gone off on a bicycle to fetch a doctor.

But it was useless. The old carter's body had scarcely been laid on the bank, motionless and apparently lifeless, before a bargee took off his jacket, knelt down beside the drowned man's huge chest, and began rhythmical traction on the tongue.

Somebody had brought the lantern. The body looked shorter and stockier than ever, the dripping mud-stained face was livid.

'He's moving! . . . I tell you he's moving!'

There was no jostling in the crowd. The silence was such that the slightest word sounded as loud as in a cathedral. And all the time a jet of water could be heard gushing from a sluice which had not been properly closed.

'Well?' asked the lock-keeper coming back.

'He's alive . . . but only just.'

'We ought to have a mirror. . . .'

The skipper of the *Providence* ran to fetch one he had on board. The man who was practising artificial respiration was dripping with sweat and another took his place, pressing harder on the drowned man.

By the time the doctor came, arriving in a motor by a

side-road, everybody could see old Jean's chest slowly rising and falling.

His jacket had been removed. The open shirt revealed a chest as hairy as any animal's. Under the right breast there was a long scar and Maigret caught a glimpse of something which looked like a tattoo-mark on the shoulder.

'Next boat!' shouted the lock-keeper cupping his hands round his mouth. 'After all, you can't do anything to help. . . .'

And one bargee moved regretfully away, calling his wife who was talking to some other women some way off.

'You haven't stopped the engine, I hope?'

The doctor asked the onlookers to move away, frowning as soon as he felt the chest.

'He's alive, isn't he?' the first life-saver asked proudly.

'I'm from Police Headquarters,' Maigret broke in. 'Is it serious?'

'Most of his ribs are broken. . . . Admittedly he's alive. . . . But I'd be surprised if he lived for long. . . . Was he trapped between a couple of boats?'

'Probably between a boat and the lock.'

'Feel here . . .'

And the doctor made the Chief-Inspector feel the left arm, which was broken in two places.

'Is there a stretcher?'

The injured man gave a faint sigh.

'I'd better give him an injection in any case. . . . But have a stretcher brought here as quickly as possible. . . . The hospital is a quarter of a mile away. . . .'

There was a stretcher in the lock-keeper's house, in accordance with regulations, but it was in the attic, where, through the skylight, the flame of a candle could be seen moving about.

The skipper's wife was sobbing at some distance from Maigret, whom she was looking at reproachfully.

Ten men lifted the carter, who gave a fresh groan. Then a lantern moved away in the direction of the main road, shedding a halo around a compact group of men, while a motor-barge, showing its green and red navigation lights, sounded its hooter three times and went to moor in the middle of the town, so as to be the first to leave the next day.

*

Ward 10. It was purely by chance that Maigret saw the number. There were only two patients there, one of whom was wailing like a baby.

The Chief-Inspector spent most of the time pacing up and down the white-paved corridor, with nurses running by and passing on orders in an undertone.

In Ward 8, opposite, which was full of women, questions were being asked about the new patient and forecasts made.

'If they've put him in Ward 10! . . .'

The doctor was a plump man wearing horn-rimmed spectacles. He went past two or three times, in his white coat, without saying anything to Maigret.

It was nearly eleven o'clock when he finally came up to him.

'Do you want to see him?'

It was a baffling sight. The Chief-Inspector could hardly recognize old Jean, who had at last been shaved so that two cuts he had suffered on the cheek and the forehead could be treated.

There he was, all clean, in a white bed, in the neutral light of a lamp with a frosted-glass chimney.

The doctor drew back the sheet.

'Look at that carcass! . . . He's built like a bear. . . . I don't think I've ever seen a body like that. . . . How did he get smashed up?'

'He fell off the lock-gate while the sluices were open. . . .'

'I see. . . . He must have been crushed between the wall and the barge. . . . The chest is literally bashed in. . . . The ribs have given way. . . .'

'The rest?'

'We'll have to examine him tomorrow, my colleagues

94

and I, if he's still alive. . . . It's a ticklish job . . . The slightest slip might kill him . . .'

'Has he recovered consciousness?'

'I just don't know. That's perhaps the most baffling thing about it. . . . Just now, when I was probing his injuries, I had a distinct impression that his eyes were half-open and that he was watching me. . . . But as soon as I looked at him he dropped his eyelids. . . . He hasn't been delirious. . . . At the very most he gives a groan now and then . . .'

'What about his arm?'

'That's nothing serious. The double fracture has already been reduced. . . . But you can't mend a chest like a humerus. . . . Where does he come from?'

'I don't know.'

'I asked you that because he's got some queer tattoo-marks. . . . I've seen those of the African Battalions, but these are different. . . . I'll show them to you tomorrow when we take the plaster off for the examination. . . .'

The porter came up to say that some people were insisting on seeing the injured man. Maigret himself went into the lodge, where he found the couple from the *Providence* who had dressed in their Sunday best.

'We can see him, can't we, Chief-Inspector? . . . It's your fault, you know. . . . You upset him with your questions. . . . Is he any better?'

'He's a little better. . . . The doctors will make their diagnosis tomorrow. . . .'

'Let me see him! . . . Even if it's only from a distance. . . . He was so much part of the boat . . .'

She did not say *of the family* but *of the boat*, and perhaps that was even more touching.

Her husband stood shyly behind her, ill at ease in a blue serge suit, his scraggy neck enclosed by a celluloid collar.

'I advise you not to make any noise. . . .'

The two of them looked at him from the corridor, from where nothing could be seen but a vague shape under the sheet, a little ivory in place of the face, a few white hairs.

95

A dozen times the skipper's wife was on the point of rushing forward.

'Look here ... If we paid something, would he be treated better?'

She did not dare to open her handbag, but fidgeted nervously with it.

'There are hospitals, aren't there, where if you pay... At least the other patients haven't got anything catching, I hope?'

'Are you staying at Vitry?'

'Why, of course we aren't going to leave without him! ... It doesn't matter about the load.... What time can we come tomorrow morning?'

'Ten o'clock,' said the doctor who had been listening impatiently.

'There isn't something we could bring him, is there? ... A bottle of champagne? Some Spanish grapes?'

'We'll give him everything he needs. ...'

And the doctor pushed them gently towards the porter's lodge. When she got there, the good woman furtively took a ten-franc note out of her bag and pressed it on the porter, who looked at her in astonishment.

*

Maigret went to bed at midnight, after wiring to Dizy to forward any messages which might arrive for him there.

At the last moment he had learnt that the *Southern Cross*, after overtaking most of the barges, had arrived at Vitry-le-François and had moored at the end of the line of waiting boats.

The Chief-Inspector had taken a room at the Hôtel de la Marne, in the town, a fairly long way from the canal, and here he found nothing of the atmosphere in which he had lived for the last few days.

The guests who were playing cards were commercial travellers.

One of them, who arrived after the others, announced: 'It seems there's been a man drowned in the lock. ...'

'Come and make up a foursome.... Lamperrière is losing like nobody's business.... Is the fellow dead?'

'I don't know.'

That was all. The manager's wife was dozing behind the cash-desk. The waiter scattered some sawdust on the floor and stoked up the stove for the night.

There was a bathroom, just one, in which the bath had lost part of its enamel. For all that, Maigret took a bath at eight o'clock the next morning, and sent the waiter to buy him a new shirt and a collar.

But as time went by he began to lose patience. He was in a hurry to see the canal again. When he heard a siren he asked:

'Is that for the lock?'

'For the lift-bridge.... There are three of them in the town....'

It was a grey, windy day. He could not remember how to get to the hospital and had to ask his way several times, for every street brought him back without fail to the market place.

The porter recognized him and came to meet him, exclaiming:

'You'd never have believed it, would you?'

'What?... Is he alive?... Is he dead?'

'You mean you don't know? The director has just phoned to your hotel...'

'Tell me quick...'

'Well, he's gone.... Done a flit.... The doctor swears that it's impossible, that he couldn't have gone a hundred yards in the state he was in.... All the same, he's vanished....'

Maigret heard some voices in the garden, behind the building, and rushed in that direction.

He found an old man whom he had not seen before and who was the director of the hospital. He was speaking sternly to the doctor whom Maigret had seen the previous day and to a red-haired nurse.

'I swear that's the truth!' the doctor was saying. 'You know as well as I do what it's like. . . . When I say ten broken ribs it's probably an underestimate. . . . Not to mention the drowning and the shock. . . .'

'How did he get out?' asked Maigret.

They showed him the window, which was about five feet above the ground. In the earth could be seen the marks of two bare feet, as well as a long trail which suggested that the carter had fallen headlong straight away.

'There you are! . . . The nurse, Mademoiselle Berthe, spent the night in the duty-room as usual. . . . She didn't hear anything. . . . About three o'clock she had to attend to a patient in Ward 8, and she glanced into Ward 10. . . . The lamps were out. . . . Everything was quiet. . . . She can't say whether the man was still in bed. . . .'

'What about the other two patients?'

'One of them has to have an emergency operation. . . . We're waiting for the surgeon. . . . The other didn't wake up at all during the night. . . .'

Maigret's eyes followed the tracks, which led to a flower bed where a little rose-bush had been trampled on.

'Is the gate always left open?'

'This isn't a prison!' retorted the director. 'And how can we foresee that a patient is going to jump out of the window? . . . Only the main door of the building was locked, as usual. . . .'

Outside, there was no point in looking for tracks, for there was a paved road. In between a couple of houses could be seen the double line of trees along the canal.

'The fact is,' added the doctor, 'I was practically sure that we should find him dead this morning. . . . And seeing that there was nothing to be done. . . . That's why I put him in Ward 10. . . .'

He was somewhat truculent, for he was still smarting from the reproaches the director had levelled at him.

Maigret walked round and round the garden for a while

like a circus horse, and suddenly, touching the brim of his bowler hat by way of farewell, he set off for the lock.

The *Southern Cross* was just entering it. Vladimir, with the skill of a real seaman, tossed the loop of a rope over a bitt and brought the boat to a dead stop.

As for the colonel, dressed in long oilskins and his white cap, he was standing impassively at the little wheel.

'The gates!' shouted the lock-keeper.

There were only about twenty boats left to lock through.

'Is it her turn?' asked Maigret, pointing to the yacht.

'It is and it isn't. . . . If you regard her as a *motor-vessel* she has precedence over a *horse-boat*. . . . But as a *pleasure-craft*. . . . Still, we get so few of them we aren't very strict about the regulations. . . . And as they tipped the bargees. . . .'

It was the latter who were working the sluices.

'Where's the *Providence*?'

'She was blocking the way. . . . This morning she went and moored on the bend, a hundred yards farther on, just before the second bridge. . . . Have you any news of the old man? . . . I'll probably have to pay dearly for that business. . . . But I'd like to see you manage any other way. . . . Strictly speaking, I ought to do the locking through myself. . . . But if I did, there'd be a hundred boats waiting every day. . . . . Four gates! . . . Sixteen sluices! . . . and have you any idea how much I'm paid? . . .'

He had to move away for a moment, because Vladimir was holding out his papers and a tip.

Maigret took the opportunity to walk off along the canal. At the bend he caught sight of the *Providence*, which by now he could have recognized among a hundred barges.

A little smoke was coming out of the chimney; there was nobody on deck; all the hatches were closed.

He nearly went up the after-gangway, leading to the bargees' quarters.

Then he changed his mind and climbed the wide gangway which was used to take the horses on board.

One of the hatches covering the stable had been removed.

The head of one of the horses was poking out, sniffing the wind.

Looking inside, Maigret made out a dark figure stretched out on the straw behind the animal's legs. And, close to it, the skipper's wife was squatting with a bowl of coffee in her hand.

In a curiously gentle, motherly voice, she was murmuring:

'Come along, Jean. . . . Drink it while it's hot! . . . It'll do you good, you old silly. . . . Do you want me to lift up your head?'

But the man lying beside her did not move but gazed at the sky.

Against that sky was silhouetted Maigret's head, which he must have seen.

And the Chief-Inspector had the impression that across the face, which was criss-crossed with sticking-plaster, there passed a happy, ironic, even truculent smile.

The old carter tried to lift his hand to push away the cup the woman was holding to his lips. But it fell limply by his side, wrinkled, horny, and speckled with little blue spots which must have been the vestiges of old tattoo-marks.

CHAPTER 9

The Doctor

'You see? He's dragged himself home like a wounded dog. . . .'

Had the woman any idea of the injured man's condition? In any case she was not panicking. She was as calm as if she were nursing a child down with influenza.

'Coffee can't do him any harm, can it? . . . But he won't drink any. . . . It must have been four in the morning when my husband and I were woken up by a tremendous noise on board. . . . I took the revolver . . . I told him to follow me with the lantern. . . .

'Believe it or not, Jean was there, looking pretty much as he is now. . . . He must have fallen from the deck. . . . That's about a six-foot drop. . . .

'To begin with, we couldn't see very clearly . . . I thought for a moment he was dead. . . .

'My husband wanted to call some of our neighbours to help lift him on to a bed. . . . But Jean understood . . . he started squeezing my hand . . . squeezing it so hard! . . . It was as if he was hanging on to it like grim death. . . .

'And I could see him sniffing. . . .

'I understood. . . . Because in the eight years he's been with us, you know . . . He can't talk . . . but I think he can hear what I'm saying. . . . Am I right, Jean? . . . Are you in pain?'

It was difficult to know whether the injured man's eyes were shining with intelligence or fever.

The woman brushed away a piece of straw which was touching his ear.

'Me, you know, my life's my little household, my brasses, my bits and pieces of furniture . . . I do believe that if somebody gave me a palace, I'd be downright un-happy. . . .

'For Jean, it's his stable . . . and his horses. . . . How can I explain? . . . There are naturally days when we don't move because we're unloading. . . . Jean has got nothing to do . . . he could go to the pub. . . .

'But no! He lies down here. . . . He leaves an opening for a ray of sunlight to come in. . . .'

And Maigret imagined himself where the carter was, seeing the partition coated with resin on his right, with the whip hanging on a twisted nail, the tin cup hooked on to another, a patch of sky between the boards above, and on the right the horses' muscular croppers.

The whole scene gave off an animal warmth, a sensation of full-blooded life which took one by the throat like the harsh wine of certain hill-sides.

'He can be left here, can't he?'

She beckoned to the Chief-Inspector to follow her out-side. The lock was working at the same rhythm as the day before. And all around were the streets of the town, with their bustling life which had nothing to do with the canal.

'He's going to die after all, isn't he? . . . What has he done? . . . You can tell me, you know . . . but you must admit that I couldn't say anything. . . . In the first place, I don't know anything. . . . Once, and only once, my hus-band found Jean with his chest bare. . . . He saw the tattoo-marks . . . not like those some sailors wear. . . . We guessed what you would have guessed. . . .

'I think I felt fonder than ever of him after that. . . . I told myself that he probably wasn't what he seemed to be, that he was hiding . . .

'I wouldn't have questioned him for all the money in the world. . . . You don't think he killed the woman, do you . . . or if he did, well, I'm sure she deserved it. . . .

'Jean . . . Jean is . . .'

She searched for a word which would express what she meant, but failed to find one.

'Ah, there's my man getting up. . . . I packed him off to bed, because he's never been very strong in the chest. . . . Do you think if I made a really strong soup . . .?'

'The doctors will be coming. In the meantime it would be better. . . .'

'Have they got to come? . . . They're going to make him suffer, spoil his last moments which . . .'

'It's absolutely essential . . .'

'He's so happy here with us. . . . Can I leave you for a minute? . . . You won't bother him, will you? . . .'

Maigret gave a reassuring nod, went back into the stable, and took out of his pocket a metal box containing a little pad soaked in oily ink.

It was still impossible to tell whether the carter was conscious. His eyelids were half-open. Between them there filtered a serene, neutral gaze.

But when the Chief-Inspector picked up the injured man's right hand and pressed his fingers on to the pad, one after another, he had the impression that for a split-second at the most the shadow of a smile touched his lips again.

He took the finger-prints on a sheet of paper, looked at the dying man for a moment, as if he were hoping for something, threw a last glance at the partitions and at the croppers of the two horses which were showing signs of impatience, and went out.

Beside the helm, the skipper and his wife were having their breakfast of bread and coffee and looking in his direction. Less than five yards from the *Providence*, the *Southern Cross* was moored, with nobody on deck.

The day before, Maigret had left his bicycle at the lock, where he found it waiting for him. Ten minutes later he was at the police station, sending a motor-cyclist to Épernay with instructions to transmit the finger-prints to Paris by the Belin telephotograph.

When he came back on board the *Providence*, he was accompanied by two doctors from the hospital with whom he was soon involved in an argument.

The doctors wanted to take their patient back to hospital. The skipper's wife, thoroughly alarmed, threw beseeching glances at Maigret.

'Can you cure him?'

'No. The chest has been smashed in. One rib has entered the right lung. . . .'

'How long has he got to live?'

'Anybody else would be dead already . . . He might last another hour, another five . . .'

'In that case, leave him here.'

The old man had not moved, had not stirred a muscle. As Maigret passed the skipper's wife, she touched his hand shyly, in a gesture of gratitude.

The doctors looked disgruntled as they crossed the gangway.

'Allowing him to die in a stable!' grumbled one of them.

'Oh, what does it matter? . . . After all, he was allowed to live in it . . .'

All the same, the Chief-Inspector stationed a policeman close to the barge and the yacht, with instructions to inform him if anything happened.

From the lock he telephoned to the Café de la Marine at Dizy, and was told that Inspector Lucas had just been in and that he had hired a taxi at Épernay to drive him to Vitry-le-François.

There followed a long, empty hour. The skipper of the *Providence* took advantage of this respite to tar the dinghy he had in tow. Vladimir polished the brasses on the *Southern Cross*.

As for the woman, she was seen constantly crossing the deck, going from the kitchen to the stable. Once she was carrying a pillow of dazzling whiteness, another time a bowl of steaming liquid, presumably the soup she had insisted on making.

About eleven o'clock Lucas arrived at the Hôtel de la Marne, where Maigret was waiting for him.

'How are you, old man?'

'All right. But you look tired, Chief . . .'

'Did your inquiries produce any results?'

'Not much. At Meaux nothing, except that the yacht created a minor scandal. The bargees couldn't sleep on account of the music and singing, and threatened to break everything up . . .'

'Was the *Providence* there?'

'She took on a load less than twenty yards from the *Southern Cross* . . . But nobody noticed anything special . . .'

'And in Paris?'

'I saw the two girls again. . . . They admitted that it wasn't Mary Lampson who had given them the necklace, but Willy Marco. . . . I got confirmation of that at the hotel, where the staff recognized her photo and hadn't seen Mrs Lampson . . . I'm not sure, but I think that Lia Lauwenstein knew Willy more intimately than she likes to admit, and that she had already helped him at Nice. . . .'

'And at Moulins?'

'Not a thing! I went to see the baker's wife, who is indeed the only Marie Dupin in the place. . . . A nice, respectable body who can't understand what's going on and keeps complaining that this business will damage her reputation. . . . The copy of the birth certificate was made eight years ago. . . . Now there's been a new Town Clerk for the last three years and his predecessor died last year. . . . They've hunted through the archives without finding anything concerning that document. . . .'

After a pause Lucas asked:

'How about you?'

'I don't know yet. . . . Nothing . . . or everything . . . I shall know any time now. . . . What are people saying at Dizy?'

'That if the *Southern Cross* hadn't been a yacht, she wouldn't have been allowed to leave, and that Mrs Lampson wasn't the colonel's first wife. . . .'

Maigret said no more, but led his companion through the streets of the little town as far as the post office.

'Get me the Police Records Office in Paris. . . .'

The telephotograph of the carter's finger-prints ought to have reached the Prefecture nearly two hours before. After that it was a matter of luck. The card corresponding to the finger-prints could be found straight away, among eighty thousand others, just as the search could last for hours.

'Take an earphone, old man . . . Hullo . . . Who's that speaking? . . . Is it you, Benoît? . . . Maigret here . . . Did you get my message? . . . What's that you say? . . . It was you who looked for the file? . . . Wait a minute . . .'

He left the call-box and went over to the counter.

'I may need the line for a long time. Make sure that I'm not cut off on any account. . . .'

When he picked up the receiver again, his eyes were brighter.

'Sit down Benoît, because I want you to read me the whole file . . . Lucas is here beside me and he'll take notes. . . . Fire away. . . .'

He could picture Benoît as clearly as if he had been in front of him, for he knew the rooms, up in the attics of the Palais de Justice, where steel cabinets contain the cards of all the criminals of France and a good many foreign law-breakers too.

'First of all his name . . . .'

'Jean Évariste Darchambaux, born at Boulogne, now aged fifty-five . . .'

Maigret automatically tried to recall a case of that name, but already Benoît's unemotional voice, pronouncing each syllable distinctly, was droning on, with Lucas writing everything down.

'Doctor of Medicine . . . Married at twenty-five to a certain Céline Mornet of Étampes . . . Settled at Toulouse, where he had done his medical training. . . . A fairly hectic life. . . . Can you hear me, Chief-Inspector?'

'Yes, very well indeed. Go on. . . .'

'I got the whole file out, because the record-card says hardly anything. . . . The couple were soon up to their necks in debt. . . . Two years after his marriage, at twenty-seven, Darchambaux was accused of having poisoned his aunt, Julia Darchambaux, who had come to live with the couple at Toulouse and disapproved of her nephew's way of life. . . . The aunt was a wealthy woman. . . . The Darchambaux were the sole heirs. . . .

'The police investigation lasted eight months, because no positive proof could be found. . . . The murderer maintained – and he was backed up by a number of experts – that the medicine prescribed for the old woman was not a poison in itself and that it was simply a case of a bold, unorthodox treatment. . . .

'There was considerable argument on the subject. . . . You don't want me to read the reports, do you? . . .

'The trial was a stormy one and the court had to be cleared several times. . . . Most people thought that Darchambaux would be acquitted, especially after the testimony of his wife, who came and swore that her husband was innocent and that if he was sent to a penal settlement she would go and join him. . . .'

'What did he get?'

'Fifteen years' hard labour . . . Wait a minute. . . . That's all there is in our files. . . . But I've sent a dispatch-rider to the Ministry of the Interior. . . . He's just got back . . .'

They could hear him talking to somebody standing behind him, and then turning over some papers.

'Here we are . . . There isn't very much. . . . The governor of Saint-Laurent-du-Maroni wanted Darchambaux to work in one of the hospitals in the penal settlement. . . . He refused. . . . His record out there was good. . . . A docile convict. . . . Only one attempt at escape, with fifteen fellow-convicts who had incited him to join them. . . .

'Five years later a new governor attempted what he called a rehabilitation of Darchambaux, but noted straight away in his report that there was nothing in the convict who was brought before him which recalled the former intellectual, nor even the well-educated man. . . .

'Right. . . . Does this interest you? . . .

'He was given a job as a medical orderly, but asked of his own accord to be sent back to the chain-gang. . . .

'He was gentle, stubborn, silent. One of his medical colleagues, interested by his case, examined him from the mental point of view and was unable to come to a definite conclusion.

'He noted, underlining these words in red ink, that there was a sort of progressive extinction of the intellectual faculties, matched by a hypertrophy of the physical faculties.

'Darchambaux committed two thefts. On both occasions it was food that he stole, the second time from a fellow-member of the chain-gang who wounded him in the chest with a sharpened flint. . . .

'Visiting journalists advised him in vain to ask for a pardon.

'When his fifteen years were over, he stayed out there under supervision, and took a job as a groom at a saw-mill where he looked after the horses.

'At forty-five he was finished with the law. All trace of him was lost . . .'

'Is that the lot?'

'I can send you the file . . . I've only given you a summary of the contents. . . .'

'There's nothing about his wife, is there? . . . You did say that she was born at Étampes, didn't you? . . . Thank you, Benoît. . . . No need to send me the papers. . . . What you've told me is enough.'

When he came out of the call-box, followed by Lucas, he was dripping with sweat.

'Ring up the Town Hall at Étampes. They'll tell you if Céline Mornet is dead. . . . At least if she's died under that name. . . . Ring up Moulins too and ask if Marie Dupin has any relatives at Étampes. . . .'

He crossed the town without seeing anything, his hands in his pockets, and had to wait for five minutes beside the canal, because the lift-bridge was up and a heavily loaded barge was moving along at a snail's pace, dragging its flat belly along the canal bed, from which the mud was rising to the surface together with bubbles of air.

In front of the *Providence* he went up to the policeman he had posted on the tow-path.

'You can go now . . .'

He noticed the colonel pacing the deck of his yacht.

The bargee's wife came running up, much more agitated than she had been that morning, with shining furrows on her cheeks.

'It's awful, Chief-Inspector . . .'

Maigret went pale, and asked, grim-faced:

'Is he dead?'

'No . . . Don't say that. . . . Just now I was alone with him . . . Because I ought to tell you that, while he was fond of my husband too, he had a preference for me. . . .

'I'm much younger than he is. . . . Well, in spite of that, he used to consider me rather as a mother . . .

'We used to go for weeks without talking . . . Only . . . Just to give you an idea . . . Usually my husband forgets the date of my name-day . . . St Hortense's Day. . . . Well, for the last eight years, Jean has never once forgotten to give me some flowers. . . . Sometimes, when we were in the depths of the country, I wondered where he got them. . . . And that day he used to put cockades on the horses' blinkers. . . .

'Well . . . I was sitting beside him just now . . . these are probably his last hours. . . . My husband would like to take the horses out, because they aren't used to being shut in such a long time . . . .

'I won't let him, because I'm sure that Jean wants them to stay with him too . . .

'I took his big hand . . .'

She started crying, but not sobbing. She went on talking, with tears running down her blotchy cheeks.

'I don't know how it happened . . . I haven't any

109

children. . . . We had even decided to adopt one when we reached the age required by law . . .

'I told him that it was nothing, that he'd get better; that we'd try to get a load for Alsace, where the countryside is so pretty in summer . . .

'I felt his fingers squeeze mine . . . I couldn't tell him that he was hurting me . . .

'It was then that he tried to speak . . .

'Can you understand that? . . . A man like him, who only yesterday was as strong as his horses. . . . He opened his mouth and made such a tremendous effort that his veins stood out on his forehead and went all purple . . .

'And I heard a hoarse noise, like an animal cry . . .

'I begged him to keep calm. . . . But he went on trying. . . . He sat up on the straw, heaven knows how . . . and he kept on opening his mouth . . .

'Some blood came out of it and trickled down his chin. . . .

'I should have liked to call my husband. . . . But Jean was still holding me . . . he frightens me . . .

'You can't imagine what it was like . . . I tried to understand . . . I asked him if he wanted something to drink. . . . No . . . Had I to go and fetch somebody? . . .

'He was so desperate at not being able to say a word. . . . I ought to have guessed . . . I tried hard enough . . .

'What do you think it could have been that he wanted to ask me? . . . Because now he's got something torn in his throat . . . I don't know . . .

'He had a haemorrhage. Finally he gritted his teeth and lay down again, right on his broken arm. . . . It must be hurting him and yet anybody would think he couldn't feel a thing. . . .

'He just lies there gazing straight in front of him . . .

'I'd give a lot to know what he'd like before . . . before it's too late. . . .'

Maigret walked noiselessly over to the stable and looked through the open hatchway.

It was as fascinating and pathetic as the death-agony of an animal with which one has no means of communicating.

The carter's body was doubled up. He had torn away part of the surgical appliance which the doctor had fitted round his torso that night.

And, at long intervals, the whistling sound of his breathing could be heard.

One of the horses had caught a foot in its tether but was standing motionless, as if it had realized that something solemn was happening.

Maigret too hesitated. He called to mind the dead woman hidden under the straw in the stable at Dizy, and then Willy's body, floating in the canal with people in the cold morning air trying to catch it with a boat-hook.

His hand, in his pocket, felt the Y.C.F. badge and the cuff-link.

And he recalled the colonel bowing to the examining magistrate and asking in a steady voice for permission to continue his journey.

In the mortuary at Épernay, in an icy room lined with metal lockers like the vaults of a bank, two bodies were waiting, each in a numbered box.

And in Paris, two women with crudely applied make-up on their faces were probably dragging their fear with them from one bar to another.

Lucas came into sight.

'Well?' Maigret called out from a distance.

'Céline Mornet has given no sign of life at Étampes since the day she applied for the papers required for her marriage to Darchambaux.'

The Inspector looked inquisitively at Maigret.

'What's the matter?'

'Ssh!'

But Lucas glanced around him in vain: he could see nothing to justify the slightest emotion.

Then Maigret took him to the stable hatchway and showed him the figure stretched out in the straw.

The skipper's wife wondered what they were going to do. From a passing motor-boat a voice called out gaily:

'Hullo! . . . Broken down?'

She started crying again, without knowing why. Her husband came back on board with a bucket of tar in one hand and a brush in the other, and announced from the stern:

'There's something burning on the stove. . . .'

She hurried automatically to the kitchen. And Maigret said to Lucas, almost regretfully:

'Let's go down . . .'

One of the horses neighed softly. The carter did not move.

The Chief-Inspector had taken the photograph of the dead woman out of his wallet, but he did not look at it.

CHAPTER 10

The Two Husbands

'LISTEN, Darchambaux. . . .'

Maigret had said that standing up, scrutinizing the carter's face. Without even realizing what he was doing, he had taken his pipe out of his pocket, but he did not think of filling it.

Perhaps the reaction was not what he had hoped for? The fact remains that he sat down on the stable bench, bent forward, his chin in his hands, and went on in a different tone of voice:

'Listen. . . . Don't get excited . . . I know that you can't talk . . .'

An unexpected shadow passing over the straw made him raise his head, and he saw the colonel standing on the deck of the barge, at the edge of the open hatchway.

The Englishman did not move, but went on following the scene from above, his feet higher up than the heads of the three men in the stable.

Lucas kept to one side, as far as the cramped conditions allowed. Maigret, feeling a little more nervous, continued:

'You aren't going to be taken away from here. . . You understand, Darchambaux? . . . In a few minutes I shall be going . . . Madame Hortense will take my place. . . .'

It was pathetic, though it would have been hard to say exactly why. Maigret, in spite of himself, was talking almost as gently as the skipper's wife.

'First of all, I want you to answer a few questions by blinking your eyes. . . . Several people are in danger of being accused and arrested at any moment. . . . You don't want that to happen, do you? . . . In that case I need you to confirm the facts. . . .'

And, while he was talking, the Chief-Inspector did not

take his eyes off the man, or stop wondering which he had in front of him at that moment, the sometime doctor, the stubborn convict, the besotted carter, or the infuriated murderer of Mary Lampson.

The body was brutish, the features coarse. But wasn't there a new expression in the eyes, an expression from which all irony had gone?

An expression of infinite sadness.

Twice Jean tried to speak. Twice they heard a noise which resembled the groaning of an animal and beads of pink saliva appeared on the dying man's lips.

All the time Maigret could see the shadow of the colonel's legs.

'When you were transported as a young man, you were convinced that your wife would keep her promise and follow you out there. It was she whom you killed at Dizy!'

Not a movement. Nothing. The face took on a greyish hue.

'She didn't come and . . . you lost heart. . . . You . . . you tried to forget everything, even your own personality. . . .'

Maigret was talking faster, as if he were losing patience. He was in a hurry to have done with it all. Above all he was afraid of seeing Jean die in the course of this horrifying interrogation.

'You came across her again by accident, when you had become a different man. . . . That was at Meaux, wasn't it? . . .'

He had to wait quite a while before the carter obediently blinked his eyes in confirmation.

The shadow of the legs moved. The barge rocked for a moment as a motor-boat went by.

'*She* had remained the same. . . . Pretty . . . and smart . . . and gay. . . . They were dancing on the deck of the yacht. . . . You didn't think of killing her straight away . . . otherwise there was no need to take her to Dizy first. . . .'

Could the dying man still hear what he was saying?

Lying in the position he was in, he must have seen the colonel just above him. But his eyes expressed nothing. Or at least, nothing intelligible.

'She had sworn to follow you everywhere. . . . You had been in a penal settlement. . . . You were living in a stable . . . and the idea suddenly occurred to you of taking her back, just as she was, with her jewels, her make-up, her white dress, and making her share your straw. . . . Wasn't that how it was, Darchambaux?'

The eyes did not blink. But the chest rose and fell. There was another groan. Lucas, who could scarcely stand it shifted in his corner.

'That's it! I'm sure it is!' exclaimed Maigret, speaking more and more quickly, as if he were growing giddy. 'Faced with his former wife, Jean the carter, who had almost forgotten Dr Darchambaux, was visited by memories of the past . . . and a strange vengeance began to take shape in his mind. . . . A vengeance? . . . Not exactly . . . an obscure desire to bring down to his level the woman who had promised to be his for life. . . .

'And Mary Lampson lived for three days hidden in this stable, almost of her own free will. . . .

'For she was afraid . . . afraid of the ghost whom she felt to be capable of anything, who ordered her to follow him. . . .

'All the more afraid in that she was conscious of the cowardice she had shown. . . .

'She came of her own accord . . . and you, Jean, you brought her corned beef, and coarse red wine. . . . You joined her, for two nights in succession, after the endless journeys along the Marne . . .

'At Dizy. . . .'

Once again the dying man stirred. But he had no strength in him. He fell back, weak and nerveless.

'She must have revolted. . . . She could not stand that sort of life any longer. . . . You strangled her in a moment of anger, rather than allow her to leave you a second time.... You carried the corpse into the stable.... Is that right?'

He had to repeat the question five times and at last the eyelids moved.

'Yes,' they said wearily.

There was a slight noise on deck. The colonel was holding back the skipper's wife who wanted to come nearer. She obeyed, impressed by his grave expression.

'The tow-path ... Your life again along the canal.... But you were worried ... You were afraid ... For you are afraid of dying, Jean.... Afraid of being imprisoned again ... afraid of transportation.... Above all, horribly afraid of leaving your horses, your stable, your straw, your little nook which has become your world.... So one night you took the lock-keeper's bicycle ... I had questioned you.... You guessed at my suspicions ...

'You came to prowl around Dizy with the idea of doing something, anything, to divert them....

'Is that right?'

Jean was now so completely still that he might have been dead. His face no longer showed anything but boredom. All the same, his eyelids dropped once again.

'When you arrived, the *Southern Cross* was in darkness. You imagined that everybody was asleep. On the deck a sailor's cap was drying out.... You picked it up..... You went to the stable to hide it under the straw.... That was a way of changing the course of the investigation and diverting it towards the people on the yacht.

'You couldn't know that Willy Marco, who was outside by himself, and who had seen you take the cap, was following you step by step... He waited for you outside the stable, where he lost one of his cuff-links ....

'Intrigued, he followed you on your way back to the stone bridge, where you had left your bicycle ...

'Did he call out to you ... Or did you hear a noise behind you? ...

'There was a struggle.... You killed him with your

116

terrible fingers, which had already strangled Mary Lampson.
You dragged his body to the canal . . .

'Then you must have walked away with your head
down. . . . On the tow-path you saw something shining, the
Y.C.F. badge. . . . And, on the spur of the moment, knowing that the badge belonged to somebody, having seen it
perhaps in the colonel's buttonhole, you dropped it where
the struggle had taken place. . . . Answer me, Darchambaux.
That *was* how things happened, wasn't it?'

'Have you broken down, the *Providence*?' called another
bargee, whose boat passed so close that his head could be
seen gliding past, level with the hatchway.

And – a strange disturbing sight – Jean's eyes filled with
tears. He blinked his eyes rapidly, as if to admit everything
and have done with it. He heard the skipper's wife reply
from the stern, where she was waiting:

'It's Jean who's been injured . . .'

Then Maigret, standing up, went on:

'Last night, when I examined your boots, you realized
that I was bound to discover the truth. . . . You tried to
kill yourself by jumping into the lock. . . .'

But the carter was so weak and was breathing with such
difficulty that the Chief-Inspector did not even wait for a
reply. He motioned to Lucas and looked round him for the
last time.

A ray of sunshine was slanting into the stable and lighting
up the carter's left ear and a hoof of one of the horses.

Just as the two men were going out, unable to think of
anything else to say, Jean tried again to speak, making a
violent effort, without regard to the pain he was suffering.
He pulled himself up into a sitting position, his eyes glaring
wildly.

Maigret did not give his attention straight away to the
colonel. He beckoned the woman, who was looking at him
from a distance.

'Well? . . . How is he?' she asked.

'Stay with him . . .'

'Can I? . . . You won't come again and . . .'

She did not dare to finish what she was saying. She had frozen into immobility on hearing the vague appeals of Jean, who seemed to be afraid of dying all alone.

Then all of a sudden she ran towards the stable.

*

Vladimir, sitting on the capstan of the yacht, with a cigarette between his lips and his white cap cocked over one ear, was splicing a rope.

A policeman was waiting on the quayside and Maigret asked him from the barge:

'What is it?'

'The answer has come from Moulins . . .'

He held out a note which said simply:

The baker's wife Marie Dupin states that she used to have a distant cousin at Étampes called Céline Mornet.

Then Maigret looked the colonel up and down. He was wearing his white cap with the big crest. His eyes were only just turning sea-green, which probably meant that he had drunk comparatively little whisky.

'You were suspicious about the *Providence*, were you?' the Chief-Inspector asked him point-blank.

It was so obvious. Wouldn't Maigret too have suspected the barge if his suspicions had not fallen for a moment on the yacht's company?

'Why didn't you say anything to me?'

The answer was worthy of the conversation between Sir Walter and the examining magistrate at Dizy.

'I wanted to settle the matter myself . . .'

And that was enough to express the colonel's contempt for the police.

'My wife?' he asked almost immediately.

'As you said yourself, as Willy Marco said, she was a charming woman . . .'

118

Maigret was not being sarcastic. Besides, he was paying more attention to the noises coming from the stable than to this conversation.

He could hear the soft murmur of a single voice, that of the skipper's wife, who sounded as if she were comforting a sick child.

'When she married Darchambaux she already had a hankering after luxury ... And it was probably for her sake that the poor doctor he was helped his aunt to die. ... I'm not saying that she abetted him. ... I'm saying that he did it for her sake ... and she was so well aware of this that she swore in the Assize Court that she would go and join him. ...

'A charming woman ... Which isn't the same thing as a heroine ...

'Her love of life proved stronger ... You must understand that, colonel. ...'

There was sunshine, wind, and threatening clouds all at once. It could start raining at any moment. The light was doubtful.

'It's so rare for men to come back from transportation ... She was pretty ... All the pleasures of life were within her reach. ... The only obstacle was her name ... So, on the Côte d'Azur, where she had met an admirer who was ready to marry her, she hit on the idea of writing to Moulins for a copy of the birth certificate of a little cousin of hers whom she remembered ...

'It's easy! So easy that there's talk at the moment of taking the finger-prints of new-born children and putting them on the registers of births ...

'She divorced her husband ... She became your wife. ...

'A charming woman ... No harm in her, I'm sure of that. ... But she liked life, didn't she? ... She liked youth, love, luxury ...

'But at the same time, every now and then, she suffered a pang of remorse which sent her out on some inexplicable escapade ...

'You know, I'm convinced that she followed Jean not so much because of his threats as from a longing to win his forgiveness. . . .

'The first day, hidden in the stable on this boat, among all the strong smells, she must have felt a vague satisfaction at the idea that she was atoning for her treachery. . . .

'The same satisfaction she felt in the Assize Court, when she cried out to the jury that she would follow her husband to Guiana.

'Charming creatures, whose first impulse is always good, even theatrical. . . . They are full of good intentions. . . .

'The trouble is that life, with its acts of cowardice, its compromises, its insistent needs, is stronger . . .'

Maigret had spoken rather heatedly, listening all the time to the sounds in the stable while his eyes followed the movements of the boats entering or leaving the lock.

The colonel stood in front of him with his head bowed. When he raised it again, it was to look at Maigret with obvious liking, and perhaps even with suppressed emotion.

'Will you come and have a drink?' he said, pointing to his yacht.

Lucas stood a little way off.

'You'll let me know, won't you?' the Chief-Inspector said to him.

There was no need for explanations between them. The inspector had understood and prowled silently round the stable.

The *Southern Cross* was as shipshape as if nothing had happened. There was not a single speck of dust on the mahogany walls of the cabin.

In the centre of the table there was a bottle of whisky, a siphon, and some glasses.

'Stay outside, Vladimir.'

Maigret was conscious of a novel impression. This time he had not come here in an attempt to discover some particle of truth. He was less clumsy, less abrupt.

And the colonel treated him as he had treated Monsieur de Clairfontaine de Lagny.

'He's going to die, isn't he?'

'Yes, any minute now. . . . He's known that since yesterday. . . .'

The soda-water spurted from the siphon. Sir Walter said solemnly:

'Your health!'

And Maigret drank, just as thirstily as his host.

'Why did he leave the hospital?'

The rhythm of the answers was slow. Before replying, the Chief-Inspector looked around him, noting the smallest details of the cabin.

'Because . . .'

He searched for his words, while his companion was already filling the glasses again.

'. . . a man without any ties . . . a man who has cut all links with his past, with his former personality . . . He has to have something to hang on to! . . . And that something is his stable . . . the smell . . . the horses . . . the scalding-hot coffee gulped down at three in the morning before walking all day. . . . His lair, if you like . . . his own nook. . . . Full of his animal warmth. . . .'

And Maigret looked the colonel in the eyes. He saw him turn his head away. He added, picking up his glass:

'There are all sorts of lairs. . . . There are some which smell of whisky, eau-de-Cologne, women . . . With a gramophone playing and . . . .'

He stopped talking to have a drink. When he raised his head again, his companion had had time to empty a third glass.

And Sir Walter was looking at him with his big, bleary eyes, and holding out the bottle.

'No, thank you,' protested Maigret.

'Yes . . . I need . . .'

Wasn't there a certain affection in his gaze?

'My wife . . . Willy . . .'

At that moment a startling thought crossed the Chief-Inspector's mind. Wasn't Sir Walter just as lonely, just as helpless as Jean, who was dying in his stable?

And then the carter had his horses beside him, and his skipper's motherly wife.

'Have another . . . I insist. . . . You're a gentleman . . .'

He was almost begging Maigret to accept. He was holding out his bottle with a rather shame-faced expression. Vladimir could be heard walking up and down the deck.

Maigret held out his glass. But there was a knock on the door. Lucas called out.

'Chief-Inspector!'

And with the door only half-open he added:

'It's all over! . . .'

The colonel did not move. He watched the two men walk away with a morose expression on his face. When Maigret turned round he saw him empty at one gulp the glass he had just filled, and heard him shout:

'Vladimir!'

Near the *Providence* a few people had collected, for sobbing could be heard from the bank.

It was Hortense Canelle, the skipper's wife, who was kneeling beside Jean and still talking to him, even though he had been dead for several minutes.

Her husband, on the deck, was watching for Maigret to arrive. He hurried over to him, a thin agitated figure, and murmured despairingly:

'What shall I do? . . . He's dead . . . My wife . . .'

A sight Maigret would never forget: in the stable, seen from above, and encumbered by the two horses, a body almost curled up into a ball, with half the head buried in the straw. And the woman's fair hair catching the sunlight while she groaned softly, murmuring every now and then:

'My little Jean . . .'

As if Jean had been a child and not that old man, hard as granite, with a gorilla's body, who had baffled the doctors.

CHAPTER II

Overtaking

NOBODY noticed except Maigret. Two hours after Jean's death, while the body was being carried on a stretcher to a waiting ambulance, the colonel, with bloodshot eyes, but a dignified bearing, had asked:

'Do you think they'll give me the burial permit?'

'Tomorrow, yes. . . .'

Five minutes later, Vladimir, with his usual precise movements, was casting off the mooring-ropes.

Two boats were waiting outside the lock at Vitry-le-François, on their way towards Dizy.

The first was already being punted into position when the yacht brushed past her, went round her curved bow, and entered the open lock.

There were cries of protest. The bargee shouted to the lock-keeper that it was his turn, that he would make an official complaint, and a great deal besides.

But the colonel, in his white cap and officer's uniform, did not even turn round.

He stood at the brass wheel, impassive, looking straight ahead.

When the lock-gates were closed, Vladimir went ashore, presented his papers, gave the traditional tip.

'Well, I'll be damned! Those yachts can get away with anything!' grumbled a carter. 'With ten francs at every lock . . .'

The canal-reach below Vitry-le-François was crowded. It scarcely seemed possible for the yacht even to punt its way between the boats waiting their turn.

And yet the gates were hardly open before the water started bubbling round the propeller. With a casual movement the colonel moved the gear-lever forward and let in the throttle.

And at one go the *Southern Cross* reached her full speed, passed close to the heavy barges, in the midst of shouts of protest, but did not touch a single one.

Two minutes later she disappeared round the bend and Maigret said to Lucas, who had accompanied him:

'They are both dead-drunk!'

Nobody had guessed. The colonel was dignified and correct, with the huge gold crest in the centre of his cap.

Vladimir, in a striped jersey, with his forage cap on the top of his head, had not made a single false move.

But if Sir Walter's apoplectic neck was purple, his face was sickly pale, his eyes underlined with heavy pouches, his lips colourless.

As for the Russian, the slightest shock would have thrown him off his balance, for he was asleep on his feet.

On board the *Providence* everything was closed and silent. The two horses, a hundred yards from the barge, were tied to a tree.

And the skipper and his wife had gone off into the town to order mourning clothes.

MORE ABOUT PENGUINS

Penguinews, which appears every month, contains details of all the new books issued by Penguins as they are published. From time to time it is supplemented by *Penguins in Print*, which is a complete list of all books published by Penguins which are in print. (There are well over four thousand of these.)

A specimen copy of *Penguinews* will be sent to you free on request. For a year's issues (including the complete lists) please send 30p if you live in the United Kingdom, or 60p if you live elsewhere. Just write to Dept EP, Penguin Books Ltd, Harmondsworth, Middlesex, enclosing a cheque or postal order, and your name will be added to the mailing list.

Note: *Penguinews* and *Penguins in Print* are not available in the U.S.A. or Canada

MARGERY ALLINGHAM

POLICE AT THE FUNERAL

Starring Albert Campion, bland, blue-eyed, deceptively vague professional adventurer, and Great Aunt Caroline, that formidable and exquisite old lady, ruling an ancient household heavy with evil.

Uncle Andrew is dead, shot through the head. Cousin George, the black sheep, is skulking round corners. Aunt Julia is poisoned. Uncle William attacked. And terror invades an old Cambridge residence.

Also available

BLACK PLUMES

CARGO OF EAGLES

THE CRIME AT BLACK DUDLEY

MR CAMPION AND OTHERS

MORE WORK FOR THE UNDERTAKER

THE TIGER IN THE SMOKE

SIMENON

'The best living detective-writer . . . Maigret is the very bloodhound of heaven' – C. Day Lewis in a broadcast

SOME OF THE SIMENON CRIME AVAILABLE IN PENGUINS:

MAIGRET MEETS A MILORD

MAIGRET AND THE HUNDRED GIBBETS

MAIGRET AND THE ENIGMATIC LETT

MAIGRET STONEWALLED

MAIGRET AT THE CROSSROADS

MAIGRET MYSTIFIED

THE SIXTH SIMENON OMNIBUS*

*NOT FOR SALE IN THE U.S.A. OR CANADA